THE BLACK NOTEBOOK

THE BLACK NOTEBOOK

A NOVEL BY
PATRICK MODIANO

Translated from the French by
Mark Polizzotti

MACLEHOSE PRESS
QUERCUS · LONDON

First published in the French language as *L'herbe des nuits* by
Editions Gallimard, Paris, in 2012
First published in Great Britain in 2016 by MacLehose Press
This paperback edition published in 2017 by

MacLehose Press
An imprint of Quercus Publishing Ltd
Carmelite House
50 Victoria Embankment
London EC4Y 0DZ

An Hachette UK company

A CIP catalogue record for this book is available
from the British Library.

ISBN (MMP) 978 0 85705 488 3
ISBN (Ebook) 978 0 85705 490 6

10 9 8 7 6 5 4 3 2 1

Designed and typeset in Albertina by Libanus Press, Marlborough
Printed and bound in Great Britain by Clays Ltd, St Ives plc

AND YET, IT WAS NO DREAM. SOMETIMES I CATCH myself saying those words in the street, as if hearing someone else's voice. A toneless voice. Names come back to me, certain faces, certain details. No-one left to talk with about it. One or two witnesses must still be alive. But they've probably forgotten the whole thing. And in the end, I wonder whether there really were any witnesses.

No, it wasn't a dream. The proof is that I still have this black notebook full of my jottings. I need precise words in this haze, so I look in the dictionary. "Note: A short piece of writing that is used to help someone remember something." The pages of my notebook contain a succession of names, telephone numbers, appointments and also short texts that might have something to do with literature. But what category should they be listed under? Private journal? Fragments of a memoir?

And also hundreds of classified ads copied down from newspapers. Lost dogs. Furnished flats. Employments sought and offered. Psychics.

Among those masses of notes, some have stronger resonance than others. Especially when nothing disturbs the silence. The telephone stopped ringing long ago. And no-one will knock at the door. They must think I'm dead. You are alone, concentrating, as if trying to capture Morse code signals being sent from far away by an unknown correspondent. Naturally, many signals are garbled, and no matter how hard you strain your ears they are lost forever. But a few names stand out clearly in the silence and on the empty page...

Dannie, Paul Chastagnier, Aghamouri, Duwelz, Gérard Marciano, "Georges", the Unic Hôtel, rue du Montparnasse... As I remember it, I always felt on my guard in that neighbourhood. The other day, I happened to walk through it. I had a strange sensation. Not that time had passed, but that another me, a twin, was prowling around there, a me who hadn't aged, and who was still living – down to the smallest detail, and until the end of time – through what I had experienced over a very short period.

What caused the unease I felt back then? Was it those few

streets in the shadow of a railway station and a graveyard? Now they struck me as harmless. Their façades had changed colour. Lighter. Nothing special. A neutral zone. Could I possibly have left behind a double, someone who would repeat each of my former movements, follow in my old footsteps, for all eternity? No, nothing remained of us here. Time had wiped the slate clean. The area was brand-new, sanitised, as if it had been rebuilt on the site of a condemned block. And even though most of the buildings were still the same, they made you feel as if you were looking at a taxidermied dog, a dog you had once owned, that you had loved when it was alive.

That Sunday afternoon, on my walk, I tried to recall what was written in the black notebook, which I regretted not having with me. Times of appointments with Dannie. The telephone number of the Unic Hôtel. The names of the people I met there. Chastagnier, Duwelz, Gérard Marciano. Aghamouri's number at the Moroccan Pavilion at the Cité Universitaire. Short descriptions of different areas in that neighbourhood, for a piece I planned to call "L'Arrière-Montparnasse", until I discovered thirty years later that the title had already been used by a certain Oser Warszawski.

One late Sunday afternoon in October, then, my footsteps had led me to that neighbourhood, which I would have avoided any other day of the week. No, it wasn't really a pilgrimage. But Sundays, especially in late afternoon, if you are alone, open a breach in time. You need only slip into it. A stuffed dog that you loved when it was alive. The moment I walked past the large, dirty white-and-beige building at 11 rue d'Odessa – I was on the opposite pavement, the one on the right – I felt something click, the slight dizziness that seizes you whenever time splits open. I stood frozen, staring at the façades that enclosed the small courtyard. That was where Paul Chastagnier always used to park his car, when he lived in a room on rue du Montparnasse, at the Unic Hôtel. One evening, I had asked why he didn't just leave the car in front of the hotel. He had given me a guilty half-smile and answered with a shrug, "As a precaution . . ."

A red Lancia. It could easily draw attention. But then, if he wanted to remain invisible, why on earth choose that colour or make of car? Besides, he had said, a friend of his lived in this building on rue d'Odessa and he often lent him the car. Yes, that's why it was parked there.

"As a precaution," he said. I had soon realised that this man, in his forties, dark-haired, always immaculately dressed in grey suits and navy-blue overcoats, did not hold any particular profession. I heard him make phone calls at the Unic Hôtel, but the wall was too thick for me to follow the conversation.

Only the sound of his voice reached me: deep, sometimes sharp. Long pauses. I had got to know this Chastagnier at the Unic Hôtel, along with several others I met in the same establishment: Gérard Marciano, Duwelz, whose first name I don't recall ... Their outlines have grown hazy with time, their voices inaudible. Paul Chastagnier stands out more clearly because of the colours: black hair, navy-blue overcoat, red car. I imagine he served time in prison, like Duwelz, and like Marciano. He was the oldest of the bunch, and he has surely died since then. He got up late and held his appointments far away from there, in the southern part of town, that hinterland around the old freight depot, where I too knew the local street names: Falguière, Alleray, and, a bit further along, rue des Favorites ... Empty cafés where he sometimes brought me, and where he probably thought no-one could find him. I never dared ask if he was officially *persona non grata* in Paris, though the idea often crossed my mind. But then, why would he park his red car in front of those cafés? Wouldn't it have been more prudent, more discreet, to walk? At the time, I often wandered around that neighbourhood, where they were beginning to pull down the squat buildings with bricked-in windows facing areas of waste ground, leaving sections of street amid heaps of rubble, as if after a bombardment. And that red car parked there, its section of rue Vandamme still remained, surrounded by the mass of new constructions. The thought made me break out in nervous laughter. I continued to follow the corridor with its glass doors. I couldn't see the end of it and the fluorescent lights made me blink. I thought that maybe the corridor simply followed the former path of rue Vandamme. I closed my eyes. The café was at the back of the street, which was prolonged by a dead end that abutted the wall of the marshalling yard. Paul Chastagnier parked his red car in the dead end, in front of the black wall. There was a hotel above the café, the Hôtel Perceval, named after a nearby street, it too erased by the new construction. I had recorded all of it in the black notebook.

Towards the end, Dannie no longer felt safe at the Unic – as Chastagnier said – and she had taken a room in that Hôtel Perceval. From then on, she tried to avoid the others, without my knowing which "other" in particular: Chastagnier? Duwelz? Gérard Marciano? The more I think about it now, the more it seems her unease began on the day I first noticed a man in the foyer and behind the reception desk, a man Chastagnier said was the manager of the Unic Hôtel and whose name figures in my notebook: Lakhdar, followed by another name, Davin, in parentheses.

*

I got to know her in the cafeteria of the Cité Universitaire, where I often went to hide out. She was living in a room in the American Pavilion, and I wondered on what grounds, as she was neither a student nor American. She moved out soon after we met – maybe ten days later. I'm reluctant to divulge the family name I'd written in the black notebook the first time we spoke: Dannie R., Pavillon des Etats-Unis, 15 boulevard Jourdan. Perhaps she's going by it again these days – after so many other names – and I wouldn't want to draw attention to her, in case she's still alive somewhere. And yet, if she read that name in print, perhaps she'd remember having used it at a certain time of her life and would get in touch. But no, I'm under no illusions on that score.

On the day we met, I'd written "Dany" in my notebook. She had corrected the spelling, using my pen: "Dannie". Later, I discovered that the name Dannie was the title of a poem by a writer I admired at the time, whom I occasionally saw leaving the Hôtel Taranne on boulevard Saint-Germain. Strange co-incidences do happen.

The Sunday evening when she moved out of the American Pavilion, she had asked me to come and meet her at the Cité Universitaire. She was waiting for me in front of the pavilion with two overnight bags. She told me she had found a room in a hotel in Montparnasse. I suggested we walk. The two over-night bags weren't very heavy.

We followed avenue du Maine. It was empty, just like the other evening – also a Sunday, at the same hour. It was a Moroccan friend from the Cité Universitaire who had suggested the hotel, the friend she had introduced me to in the cafeteria at our first meeting, a fellow named Aghamouri.

We sat on a bench when we reached the street that runs alongside the cemetery. She rummaged in her overnight bags to make sure she hadn't forgotten anything. Then we continued on our way. She told me Aghamouri had taken a room in that hotel because one of the owners was Moroccan. But then, why did he also live in the Cité Universitaire? Because he was a student. And he even had a third residence in Paris. And what about her? Was she a student? Aghamouri was helping her enrol at the Censier branch of the university. She said it without much conviction, pronouncing that last sentence half-heartedly. And yet, one evening, as I recall, I accompanied her to the Censier campus by metro, in a direct line from Duroc to place Monge. A fine drizzle was falling, but we didn't mind. Aghamouri had told her to follow rue Monge, and we'd ulti-mately reached our destination: a kind of esplanade, or rather a piece of wasteland surrounded by squat, half-demolished buildings. The ground was hard-packed dirt and we had to take care to avoid puddles in the twilight. At the back, a modern skyscraper that was barely finished, still with its scaffolding . . . Aghamouri was waiting for us at the entrance, his silhouette standing out against the lights in the foyer. His eyes seemed less anxious than usual, as if it reassured him to stand in front of the Censier branch despite the wasteland and the rain. All these details return to me fitfully, in a jumble, and often the light grows dim. And this clashes with the precise indications in my notebook. Those indications serve me well; they lend coherence to images skipping so hard that the film is in danger of breaking. Oddly enough, I find it easier to understand other notes I took during that same period, concerning events I hadn't experienced that dated back to the nineteenth, or even eighteenth, century. And the names associated with those distant events – Baroness Blanche, Tristan Corbière, Jeanne Duval, among others, and also Marie-Anne Leroy, guillotined on July 26, 1794, at the age of twenty-one – sound nearer and more familiar to me than the names of my contemporaries.

That Sunday evening, when we arrived at the Unic Hôtel, Aghamouri was waiting for Dannie, sitting in the foyer with Duwelz and Gérard Marciano. That was when I met those two. They wanted us to go and see the garden behind the hotel, ourselves, sheltered at the back of the room. A black poodle would rest its chin on the bench and watch us, blinking. When I remember certain moments of my life, lines of poetry come to mind and I often try to recall the names of the authors. The café in place Monge, on those evenings, is associated with the line: "A dog's sharp claws scraping the pavement at night . . ."

We walked to Montparnasse. During these wanderings, Aghamouri divulged some rare personal information. At the Cité Universitaire, he had just been evicted from his room in the Moroccan Pavilion, though I never learned whether it was for political reasons or something else. He had a small flat someone had lent him in the 16th arrondissement, near the Maison de la Radio. But he preferred his room at the Unic Hôtel, which he had obtained thanks to the manager, "a Moroccan friend". So then, why keep the flat in the sixteenth? "My wife lives there. That's right, I'm married." And I had sensed he would tell me nothing more. Moreover, he never responded to questions. His disclosures to me – but can we really call them that? – were made on the way from place Monge to Montparnasse, between long silences, as if walking encouraged him to talk.

Something puzzled me. Was he really a student? When I'd asked his age, he had said he was thirty. Then he seemed sorry he'd told me. Could one still be a student at thirty? I didn't dare probe for fear of offending him. And Dannie? Why did she want to be a student? Was it really that easy to enrol at Censier? When I observed the two of them at the Unic Hôtel, they didn't really look like students; and the university building over near place Monge, standing half finished at the back of a no-man's-land, suddenly seemed to belong to another city, another country, another life. Was it because of Paul Chastagnier, Duwelz, Marciano, or the ones I'd seen at the hotel reception? But I never felt comfortable in that Montparnasse neighbourhood. No, really nothing cheery about those streets. As I recall, it was often raining there, whereas in my dreams I always see other areas of Paris bathed in sunshine. I think Montparnasse had fizzled out since the war. Further down the boulevard, the Coupole and the Select still shone a bit, but the neighbourhood had lost its soul. Its talent and heart were gone.

One Sunday afternoon, I was alone with Dannie at the lower end of rue d'Odessa. Rain was beginning to fall and we took cover in the lobby of the Montparnasse cinema. We found seats far to the back. It was intermission and we didn't know what film was playing. That huge, dilapidated picture palace had caused me the same malaise as the neighbouring streets. A smell of ozone floated over everything, as when you walk past a metro grating. In the audience were a few soldiers on leave; when night fell, they would take trains towards Brest or Lorient. And casual couples hid in dark corners, not watching the film. As it played, you could hear their moans and sighs, and beneath them the creaking of the seats, growing louder . . . I asked Dannie if she planned to stay in this neighbourhood much longer. No, not for long. She would have preferred a large room in the 16th arrondissement. It was quiet and anonymous out there. No-one could find you.

"Why? Are you hiding from someone?"

"No, of course not. What about you, do you like this neighbourhood?"

She seemed determined to avoid an awkward question. As for me, what could I say? Whether or not I liked this neighbourhood was irrelevant. Today it seems to me that I was living another life, inside of my daily life. Or rather, that this other life was connected to my drab everyday existence and lent it a phosphorescence and mystery that it didn't really have. Just as familiar places that you revisit many years later in dreams take on a strange aura, like mournful rue d'Odessa, or that Montparnasse cinema that smelled like the metro.

That Sunday, I walked her back to the Unic Hôtel. She was supposed to meet Aghamouri.

18

pretty much separated." The kind of sentence you overhear when walking past two people in the street. And you will never know what they were talking about. A train rushes by a station too fast for you to read the name of the town. And so, with your forehead pressed against the window, you note down other details: a passing river, the village bell tower, a black cow ruminating beneath a tree, removed from the herd. You hope that at the next station you'll be able to read the name and find out what region you're in. I never again saw any of the people who flit through the pages of this black notebook. Their presence was fleeting, and I could easily have forgotten their names. Simple encounters, perhaps accidental, perhaps not. There is a time in one's life for that, a crossroads where one can still choose from several paths. The age of encounters, as it said on the cover of a book I once found on the quays. And indeed, that same Sunday evening when I left Dannie with Aghamouri, I went walking – I'm not sure why – along the quai Saint-Michel. I walked up the boulevard, which was just as lugubrious as Montparnasse, perhaps because the weekday crowds were absent and the storefronts dark. Further up, where the street opened onto rue Monsieur-le-Prince, after the steps and the metal railing, was a large, brightly lit window, the back of a café whose front looked out on the fence surrounding the Jardin du Luxembourg. The interior of the café was dark, except for this one pane of glass behind which patrons clustered around a semicircular bar until late into the night. Among them that evening were two individuals whom I recognised in passing: Aghamouri, because of his camel overcoat, and, seated next to him on a barstool, Dannie.

I went nearer. I could have pushed open the glass door and joined them. But I was afraid I'd be intruding and held back. Didn't I always keep to the background at the time, like a spectator – I'd even say, like the man they called the "nocturnal spectator", that eighteenth-century writer whose work I loved and whose name appears several times, with glosses, in the pages of my black notebook? Paul Chastagnier, when we were together in the Falguière or Favorites neighbourhoods, had said to me one day, "It's odd . . . You listen to people very attentively . . . but your mind seems elsewhere . . ." Behind the glass, under the over-bright fluorescent lights, Dannie's hair appeared not light brown but blonde, and her skin even paler than normal, milky, with freckles. She was the only one seated on a stool. Three or four other customers were standing behind her and Aghamouri, glasses in hand. Aghamouri leaned towards her and said something in her ear. He kissed her neck. She laughed and took a sip of a drink that I recognised by its colour and because she ordered it whenever we were in a café: Cointreau.

I wondered whether I would tell her the next day that I had seen her with Aghamouri at the Café Luxembourg. I didn't yet know the exact nature of their relationship. In any event, they occupied separate rooms at the Unic Hôtel. I had tried to puzzle out what held that little band together. Apparently, Gérard Marciano was an old friend of Aghamouri's and the latter had introduced him to Dannie when they both lived at the Cité Universitaire. Paul Chastagnier and Marciano used the familiar *tu* with each other, despite their age difference, and the same for Duwelz. But neither Chastagnier nor Duwelz had met Dannie before she moved to the Unic Hôtel. Finally, Aghamouri maintained fairly close relations with the hotel manager, the aforementioned Lakhdar, who every other day came to the office behind the reception desk. He was often accompanied by a man named Davin. Those two seemed to have known Paul Chastagnier, Marciano and Duwelz for a long time. All this I recorded in my black notebook one afternoon while waiting for Dannie, as one might do crossword puzzles or doodle, to pass the time.

Later on, they questioned me about them. I had received a summons from a certain Langlais. I arrived at ten and spent a long time waiting in an office on the quai de Gesvres. Through the window, I gazed at the flower market and the black façade of the Hôtel-Dieu. A sunlit autumn morning on the quays. Langlais entered the office: brown hair, average height. Despite his large blue eyes, his manner was cold. Without even a hello, he began asking questions in a gruff voice. I think that because I kept my calm, his tone eventually softened and he realised that I wasn't really mixed up in all this. It occurred to me that there, in his office, I might have been sitting in the exact spot where Gérard de Nerval had hanged himself. If we looked around the cellars of this building, we would find a section of the former rue de la Vieille-Lanterne. I wasn't able to answer Langlais's questions very precisely. He cited the names of Paul Chastagnier, Gérard Marciano, Duwelz, Aghamouri, and wanted me to talk about my relations with them. That was when I realised how small a part they had played in my life. Walk-ons. I thought about Nerval and rue de la Vieille-Lanterne, on which they had erected the building we were in now. Did he know? I almost asked him. Several times during the interrogation, he brought up the name of one Mireille Sampierry, who allegedly "frequented" the Unic Hôtel, but I didn't know her. "Are you quite sure you never met?" The name meant nothing to me. He must have seen I wasn't lying and let it drop. I jotted down "Mireille Sampierry" in my notebook that evening, and at the bottom of the same page, I wrote, "14 quai de Gesvres. Langlais. Nerval. Rue de la Vieille-Lanterne." I was surprised he never mentioned Dannie. It was as if she had left no trace in their files. As the expression went, she had slipped through the cracks and disappeared into the woodwork. So much the better for her. The night when I'd discovered her with Aghamouri at the bar of the Café Luxembourg, after a while I couldn't make out her face in the glaring neon. She was no more than a spot of light, without relief, as in an overexposed photograph. A blank. I thought maybe she had eluded this Langlais's investigations by the same phenomenon. But I was mistaken. During a second interrogation the following week, I discovered that he knew plenty about her.

One evening when she still lived at the Cité Universitaire, I had accompanied her to the Luxembourg metro stop. She didn't want to go home alone to the American Pavilion, and she had asked me to take the metro with her. Just as we were heading down to the platform, the last train departed. We could have walked, but the prospect of following endless rue de la Santé at that hour of the night and skirting the high walls of the prison, then of Sainte-Anne hospital, made my blood run cold. She pulled me towards the start of rue Monsieur-le-Prince and we found ourselves at the semicircular bar, in the same spot she and Aghamouri had occupied a few nights before. She sat on a stool, while I remained standing. We were pressed together because of the many patrons crowding around the bar. The light was so harsh that it made me squint, and we couldn't hear ourselves talk in the hubbub around us. Then, one by one, everyone left. There remained only a single customer right at the back, sprawled over the bar, and we couldn't tell whether he was dead drunk or merely asleep. The light was still just as bright, just as strong, but it felt as if its scope had narrowed and only a single spotlight was trained on us. When we emerged into the open air, by contrast, everything was pitch black, and I felt relieved, like a moth that has escaped the attraction and searing heat of the lamp.

It was around two or three in the morning. She told me she often missed the last metro at Luxembourg, and that was why she'd noticed this café, which she called "the 66", the only one in the area open all night. Some time after being questioned by that Langlais, I was walking, very late, towards the upper end of boulevard Saint-Michel, and from a distance I saw a police van parked on the pavement, blocking the overly lit window of "the 66". They were rounding up customers. Yes, it was just what I had felt standing at the bar with Dannie that night.

Dazzled moths caught in the light, before a police raid. I think I'd even uttered the word "raid" in her ear, and she'd smiled.

In Paris at the time, at night, there were places that were too well lit, that acted as traps, and I did my best to avoid them. When I ended up in one of them, finding myself among odd customers, I was always on the alert, and cast about for the emergency exits. "You're acting like you're in Pigalle," she said. I was amazed to hear the word "Pigalle" trip so familiarly off her tongue. Outside, we skirted the fence of the Jardin du Luxembourg. And I repeated the word "Pigalle" and burst out laughing. She did too. All around us was silence. Through the fence came the rustling of trees. The Luxembourg metro stop was closed, and we'd have to wait until six o'clock for the first train. Behind us, they had turned off the lights in "the 66". We could go home on foot, and with her beside me I was ready to confront the long and sinister rue de la Santé.

On the way, we tried a shortcut and got lost in the narrow streets around the Val-de-Grâce. The silence was even deeper, and we could hear the sound of our footsteps. I wondered if we hadn't strayed far outside Paris, to some provincial town: Angers, Vendôme, Saumur, the names of towns I didn't know, whose quiet streets looked like rue du Val-de-Grâce, at the end of which a tall fence protected a garden.

She had taken my arm. In the distance we saw a light much duller than the one in "the 66", on the ground floor of a building.

A hotel. The glass door was open and the light came from the foyer, in the middle of which a dog was asleep, its chin resting on the tile floor. Towards the back, behind the reception desk, the bald-headed night porter was leafing through a magazine. There, on the pavement, I no longer had the courage to walk past the walls of the prison and the hospital and follow rue de la Santé.

I don't remember which of us led the way. In the foyer, we stepped over the dog without waking it. Room 5 was available. I remember that number, five, I who always forget room numbers, the colours of walls, furniture and curtains, as if it were preferable that my life from that time should gradually fade away. And yet, the walls of Room 5 have stuck in my memory, as have the curtains: wallpaper with light-blue patterns, and those black drapes that I later learned dated from the war and let no light filter out, following the rules of what they used to call "passive defence".

Later that night, I sensed she wanted to confide in me, but she hesitated. Why the Cité Universitaire, the American Pavilion, when she was neither a student nor American? Anyway, the truest encounters take place between two people who ultimately know nothing about each other, even at night in a hotel room. "Those people at 'the 66', earlier, they were a little strange," I said to her. "Good thing there wasn't a raid." Yes, those people around us, who talked too loudly under those glaring white lights – how had they washed up in the provincial Latin Quarter at that late hour? "You ask yourself too many questions," she whispered to me. A clock chimed every quarter-hour. The dog barked. Once more, I felt as if I were far outside Paris. I even seemed to hear, just before daybreak, the fading sound of hooves. Saumur? Many years later, one afternoon when I was walking near the Val-de-Grâce, I tried to find that hotel. I hadn't recorded its name or address in the black notebook, the way we tend not to write down the most intimate details of our lives, for fear that, once fixed on paper, they'll no longer be ours.

IN HIS OFFICE ON THE QUAI DE GESVRES, LANGLAIS
had asked me, "You're living at the Unic Hôtel, right?" He had
adopted a distracted tone, as if he already knew the answer
and expected only a simple confirmation.

"No."

"And you frequented 'the 66'?"

This time he looked me straight in the eye. I was surprised to
hear him say "the 66". Up until then, I had thought Dannie was
the only one who called it that. I, too, had occasionally given
cafés names other than their real ones, names from Paris' past,
and would say, for instance, "Let's meet at Tortoni's", or "Nine
o'clock at the Rocher de Cancale."

"The 66?" I pretended to search my memory. I again heard
Dannie saying in her hushed voice, "You're acting like you're
in Pigalle."

"'The 66' in Pigalle?" I said to Langlais, feigning puzzlement.

"Not exactly . . . It's a café in the Latin Quarter."

Maybe it would be better not to try to outsmart him.

"Oh, right! . . . I must have gone there once or twice . . ."

"At night?"

I hesitated before answering. It would have been more prudent to say "in the daytime", when the main room was open and most of the patrons gathered near the front windows facing out towards the Luxembourg fence. By day, the café was no different from any other. But why lie?

"Yes, at night."

I remembered the room plunged in darkness around us, and that narrow shaft of light at the rear, like a secret refuge after closing time. And that name, "the 66", one of those names that circulate in whispers, among initiates . . .

"Were you alone?"

"Yes, alone."

He read over a sheet on the desk, on which I seemed to make out a list of names. I was hoping that Dannie's wasn't among them.

"And you didn't know any of the regulars at 'the 66'?"

"Not one."

He kept his eyes glued to the sheet of paper. I would have

liked him to read me the names of the "regulars at the 66" and explain who all those people were. Maybe Dannie had known some of them. Or Aghamouri. Apparently, neither Gérard Marciano, nor Duwelz, nor Paul Chastagnier frequented "the 66". But I wasn't certain of anything.

"It must be a student café, like all the other ones in the Latin Quarter," I said.

"By day, yes. But not at night."

He had adopted a sharp, almost threatening, tone.

"You know," I said, trying to sound as gentle and conciliatory as possible, "I was never a 'night-time regular at the 66'."

He looked at me with his large blue eyes, and there was nothing threatening about his gaze, which seemed weary and rather benign.

"Anyway, you're not on the list."

Twenty years later, in the file that came into my possession thanks to that same Langlais – he hadn't forgotten me; so it is with sentinels who stand at every crossroads of your life – I found the list of the "regulars at the 66", topped by a certain "Willy of Les Gobelins". I'll copy it down when I have the time. And I'll also copy a few pages from the file that confirm and complete what I'd recorded in my old black notebook. Just yesterday, I walked past "the 66" to see if that part of the café still existed. I pushed open the glass door, the same one that Dannie and I had used and behind which I watched her, sitting at the bar next to Aghamouri, under those lights that were too strong and too white. I sat at the bar. It was five in the afternoon and the patrons had filled the other part of the café, the part that looks out on the Luxembourg fence. The waiter seemed surprised that I should order a Cointreau, but I did it in memory of Dannie. And to drink to the health of that "Willy of Les Gobelins", the first on the list, about whom I knew nothing.

"Do you still stay open late?" I asked the waiter.

He knitted his brow. He didn't seem to understand the question. A young man of about twenty-five.

"We close at nine every evening, sir."

"Is the café still called 'the 66'?"

I had pronounced those words in a sepulchral voice. He gave me a worried look.

"'The 66'? No, sir, we're called the Luxembourg."

I thought of the list of "regulars at the 66". Yes, I'll copy it down when I have time. But, yesterday afternoon, I recalled some of the names on that list: Willy of Les Gobelins, Simone Langelé, Orfanoudakis, Dr Lucaszek alias "Doctor Jean", Jacqueline Giloupe and one Mireille Sampierry, whom Langlais had mentioned previously.

Behind me, in the main room and outdoors, were tourists and students. At the nearest table, a group whose conversation I was distractedly following was composed of students from the engineering school. They were celebrating something, no doubt the beginning of summer holidays. They photographed each other with their iPhones in the dull, neutral light of the present. A banal afternoon. And yet, it was there, in that same spot, in the middle of the night, that the fluorescent lights had made me squint and we could barely hear ourselves talk, Dannie and I, because of the hubbub and the voices, now forever lost, of Willy of Les Gobelins and all those shadows surrounding us.

As I recall, there wasn't really much difference between "the 66" and the Unic Hôtel, or any of the other places in Paris I used to frequent at the time. A menace hovered over everything, giving life a peculiar coloration. Even when I was away from Paris. One day, Dannie asked me to go with her to a house in the country. On one page of my black notebook I had written: "Country house. With Dannie." Nothing more. On the preceding page, I read: "Dannie, avenue Victor-Hugo, building with two exits. Meet 7 p.m. at rear entrance on rue Léonard-de-Vinci."

I had waited there for her several times, always at the same hour, in front of the same entry porch. At the time, I had drawn a connection between the person to whom she "paid frequent visits" – an old-fashioned phrase I'd been surprised to hear her use – and the country house. Yes, if my memory serves, she had told me that the "country house" belonged to "the person" on avenue Victor-Hugo.

"Country house with Dannie." I hadn't recorded the name of the village. Leafing through the black notebook, I experience two contradictory feelings. If these pages are lacking in precise details, I tell myself it's because nothing surprised me back then. Youthful unconcern? But I read certain phrases, certain names, certain indications, and it seems to me I was sending out coded signals to the future. Yes, it's as if I wanted to leave clues, in black and white, that would help me clarify at some later date what I'd been living through at the time without really understanding it. Signals keyed blindly, in total confusion. And I'd have to wait years and years before I could decipher them.

On the page of the notebook where it says "Country house with Dannie" in black ink, there is also a list of villages that I added in blue ballpoint about ten years ago, when I got it into my head to find that country house. Was it in the Paris region or further out, near Sologne? I've forgotten why I chose those particular villages rather than others. I believe the sound of their names reminded me of one where we'd stopped for petrol. Saint-Léger-des-Aubées. Vaucourtois. Dormelles-sur-l'Orvanne. Ormoy-la-Rivière. Lorrez-le-Bocage. Chevry-en-Sereine. Boisemont. Achères-la-Forêt. La Selle-en-Hermoy. Saint-Vincent-des-Bois.

I had bought a Michelin road map which I've kept and that bears this designation: Paris, 150–km radius. North-South. And also an Ordnance Survey map of the Sologne region. I spent several afternoons poring over them, trying to retrace the route we'd followed in a car that Paul Chastagnier had lent us – not his red Lancia, but a more discreet vehicle, grey in colour. We left Paris via the Porte de Saint-Cloud, the tunnel and the highway. Why this westbound road when the country house was somewhere to the south, towards Sologne?

A little later, at the bottom of a page in the notebook where I had made some jottings about the poet Tristan Corbière, I discovered in tiny letters the word FEUILLEUSE, followed by a telephone number. The name of that village could easily have remained lost among the densely written notes about Corbière. Feuilleuse. 437-41-10. But of course: on one occasion I had gone to join Dannie at the country house and she'd given me the phone number. I had taken the bus at Porte de Saint-Cloud. The bus had stopped in a small town. I had telephoned Dannie from a café, and she had come to pick me up in a car – the grey car that Paul Chastagnier had lent us. The "country house" was about a dozen miles from there. I looked up where Feuilleuse was: not in Sologne, but in the Eure-et-Loir.

Four-three-seven, four-one, one-zero. The phone rings and rings with no answer, and I was surprised that after all these years the number was still in service. One evening, when I'd again dialled 437-41-10, I heard static and muffled voices. Perhaps it was one of those lines that had long been abandoned. The numbers were known only by the select few who used them to communicate in secret. I ended up making out a woman's voice, which kept repeating a phrase that I couldn't understand – a monotonous statement, like on a broken record. The voice of the talking clock? Or Dannie's voice, calling to me from another time and from that lost country house?

I consulted an old telephone directory from the Eure-et-Loir, which I had found at the Saint-Ouen flea market, dumped among hundreds of others. There were only about ten listings for Feuilleuse and that number was indeed among them, a secret cipher that would open the "Gateway to the Past". That was the title of a detective novel I'd taken from the library in present no longer counted, with its indistinguishable days in their doleful light, which must be the light of old age, when you feel as if you're merely living on. I told myself I was going to rediscover the row of trees, the white fences. The dog would come up to me slowly, along the path. I often thought that, apart from us, he was the house's only inhabitant, even its owner. Each time we returned to Paris, I would say to Dannie, "We should bring the dog with us." He stationed himself in front of the grey car to witness our departure. And then, when we were in the car and the doors had shut, he headed back towards the hut that served as woodshed, where he slept when we were away. And, each time, I was sorry to return to Paris. I had asked Dannie if we could stay longer in that house. We could, she said, but not right away. I had been mistaken or had misunderstood, there was no connection between the "person" on avenue Victor-Hugo to whom she paid frequent visits and this house. The owner – it was a woman – was abroad for the time being. She explained that she'd met her the year before when she was looking for work. But she didn't say what kind of "work". Neither Aghamouri nor any of those I referred to as the "Montparnasse gang" – Paul Chastagnier, Duwelz, Gérard Marciano, and other silhouettes whom I often saw in the foyer of the Unic Hôtel – knew about this house. "So much the better," I said. She smiled. Apparently, she felt the same way. One evening, we lit a fire and sat on the large couch in front of the fireplace, the dog at our feet, and she told me she was sorry she'd borrowed the grey car from Paul Chastagnier. And she even added that she wanted nothing more to do with those "losers". I was amazed to hear her use that term, as she normally chose her words so carefully and kept her thoughts to herself. Once again, I didn't have the curiosity to ask what her exact relation was with those "losers" and why she had taken a room at the Unic Hôtel on Aghamouri's say-so. To tell the truth, in the calm of that house protected by its curtain of trees and white fences, I no longer felt like asking any questions.

Still, one afternoon, we were coming back from a walk on the road to Moulin d'Etrelles – the names we think we've forgotten, or that we never speak for fear of becoming too emotional, suddenly resurface, and they aren't so painful after all – with the dog trotting on ahead, beneath the autumn sun. No sooner had we shut the front door behind us than we heard the sound of an engine coming closer. Dannie grabbed my hand and pulled me upstairs. In the bedroom, she signalled for me to sit and she took up position by the window. The engine shut off. A door slammed. The sound of footsteps from the gravelled part of the path. "Who is it?" I asked. She didn't answer. I slid over to another window. A large black car of American make. It looked as if someone was still behind the wheel. The doorbell buzzed. Twice. Three times. Downstairs, the dog was barking. Dannie was frozen, gripping the curtain with one hand. A man's voice: "Is anyone there? Is anyone there? Can you hear me?" A loud voice with a slight Belgian or Swiss accent, or else that international accent of people whose native language you never know, and who don't know it themselves. "Is anyone there?"

The dog barked all the harder. It had remained in the hallway and, if we hadn't shut the door properly, it could open it with its paw. I whispered, "You don't think that guy can get inside, do you?" She shook her head. She sat on the edge of the bed, arms folded. Her face expressed boredom more than fear; she was there, motionless, head lowered. And I kept thinking this fellow would wait in the sitting room and it would be hard to slip out of the house without him seeing us. But I kept my wits about me. I had often found myself in this kind of situation, avoiding people I knew because I no longer felt like talking to them. I would switch pavements when I saw them coming, or duck into a doorway and wait for them to pass by. Once I even crawled out of a window to escape from someone who had shown up unexpectedly. I knew many buildings with double exits, a list of which figured in my black notebook.

The buzzing at the door ceased. The dog stopped barking. From the window, I saw the man head back to the car parked next to the front steps. A tallish, dark-haired man, wearing a fur-lined coat. He leaned towards the lowered window and spoke with the person behind the wheel, whose face I couldn't see. Then he climbed into the car, and it rolled away down the path.

When evening fell, she told me it would be better not to turn on the lights. She drew the curtains in the sitting room and the room where we took our meals. We lit our way by candlelight. "Do you think they'll be back?" I asked. She shrugged. She told me they were surely friends of the owner's. She preferred not to see them, otherwise she'd have them "on her back". Now and then, that sort of colloquialism intruded on her refined speech. There in the twilight, with the curtains drawn, it occurred to me that we were guilty of breaking and entering. And it seemed almost normal, so accustomed was I to living without the slightest sense of legitimacy, a sense reserved for those who have had good, honest parents and belong to a well-defined social milieu. In the candlelight, we spoke in whispers so as not to be heard from outside, and she saw nothing odd about our situation, either. Without knowing much about her, I was sure we were from the same world and had things in common. But I would have been hard pressed to say what things.

For two or three nights, we didn't use the electricity. Without exactly saying so, she made me understand that she wasn't really "supposed" to be in that house. She had simply kept a key from the previous year. And she hadn't notified the "owner" that she planned to spend time there. She would have to arrange it with the caretaker, who tended the grounds and whom we would surely run into any day now. No, the house wasn't abandoned, as I had assumed. The days went by. The caretaker came in the morning, and our presence didn't seem to surprise him. A short, grey-haired man who wore corduroy trousers and a hunting jacket. She offered no explanations and he asked no questions. He even told us that if we needed anything, he could go and get it for us. Several times he took us, with the dog, to do the shopping in Châteauneuf-en-Thymerais. Or else, closer to home, in Maillebois and Dampierre-sur-Blévy. Those names lay dormant in my memory, but they hadn't been erased. And last night, a buried memory resurfaced. A few days before we left for Feuilleuse, I had accompanied her to the building on avenue Victor-Hugo. This time she asked me not to wait for her behind the building, opposite the entrance on rue Léonard-de-Vinci, but in a café a bit further down the street, on the square. She didn't know what time she would be out. I waited for her for about an hour. When she joined me, she was very pale. She ordered a Cointreau and downed it in one gulp, to give herself what she called a "shot in the arm". And she paid for our drinks with a 500-franc note that she pulled from a wad of cash secured by a red paper strip. She hadn't had that wad when we came by metro, because that afternoon we had had just enough to buy two second-class tickets.

La Barberie. Le Moulin d'Etrelles. La Framboisière. The words re-emerge, intact, like the bodies of those two fiancés found in the mountains, encased in ice, who hadn't aged in hundreds of years. La Barberie. That was the name of the house whose white, symmetrical façade I can still see, between rows of trees. Three years ago, travelling by train, I was distractedly perusing the classifieds in a newspaper, noticing that there were far fewer of them than back when I used to copy them into my black notebook. No more employments sought or offered. No more lost dogs. No more psychics. None of those messages strangers would send each other: "Martine. Call us. Yvon, Juanita and I are very worried." But one ad had caught my eye: "For sale. Vintage home. Eure-et-Loir. In hamlet between Châteauneuf and Brezolles. Park. Ponds. Stables. Call Paccardy Agency

(02-07) 33-71-22." I thought I recognised the house. I copied the ad at the bottom of the last page of my old black notebook, as a sort of conclusion. Still, those stables didn't ring a bell. There were indeed ponds – or rather, pools in which the dog used to splash about during our walks. La Barberie was the name not only of the house but also of the hamlet, of which the house must once have been the château. All around were sections of half-crumbled walls beneath the vegetation, no doubt the ruins of an old manor house and a chapel, and even, why not, of a stable. One afternoon when we were walking with the dog – it was thanks to him we discovered those ruins: he guided us towards them gradually, like a truffle hound – we were talking about all the repairs we would make, as if we owned the place. Perhaps Dannie didn't dare tell me that, centuries before, the house had actually belonged to her ancestors, the lords of La Barberie. And she had long wanted to come back to visit it in secret. At least, that's what I liked to imagine.

At La Barberie, I forgot around a hundred pages of a manuscript I was writing from the notes in my black book. Or rather, I had left the manuscript in the sitting room where I worked, thinking we'd be back the following week. But we were never able to return, and we abandoned the dog and the manuscript there forever.

I wrest page by page from my drab current existence to give it some light and shadow. This afternoon, we are in the here and now, it's raining, people and things are plunged in grey, and I'm impatiently waiting for night when everything will stand out more sharply, thanks to those same contrasts of shadow and light.

The other night, driving through Paris, I was moved by those lights and shadows, by the different varieties of street lights and lamp posts, which I felt were sending me signals from the avenues or street corners. It was the same feeling you get from staring at a lit window: a feeling of both presence and absence. Behind the glass pane the room is empty, but someone left the light on. For me, there has never been a present or a past. Everything blends together, as in that empty room where, every night, a light shines. I often dream that I've found my manuscript. I walk into the sitting room with its black-and-white tiled floor and rummage through the drawers under the bookshelves. Or else, a mysterious correspondent, whose name I can't quite make out on the envelope next to the word "sender", posts it to me. And the postmark shows the year when we used to go to that house in the country, Dannie and I. But I'm not surprised that the package took so long to arrive – for, indeed, there is no past or present. Thanks to my jottings in the black notebook, I can recall several chapters of that manuscript: one devoted to Baroness Blanche; another to Marie-Anne Leroy, guillotined on July 26, 1794, aged twenty-one; still others to the Hôtel Radziwill during the Revolution, to Jeanne Duval, to Tristan Corbière and his friends, Rodolphe de Battine and Herminie Cucchiani . . . None of those pages concerned the twentieth century, in which I was living. And yet, if I could read them again, the exact colours and smells of the nights and days when I wrote them would come back to me. Judging from what is in the black notebook, the Hôtel Radziwill in 1791 was not so different from the Unic Hôtel on rue du Montparnasse: the same dodgy atmosphere. And now that I think of it, didn't Dannie have something in common with Baroness Blanche? I had a very hard time retracing that woman's steps. One often loses sight of her, even though she appears in Casanova's *Memoirs*, which I was reading at the time, and in several police reports under Louis XV. Have police inspectors really changed since the eighteenth century? One day, Duwelz and Gérard Marciano confided to me under their breath that the Unic Hôtel was both kept under surveillance and protected by an inspector from the vice squad. He, too, surely wrote reports. And, more than twenty years later, among the documents in the file that Langlais gave me – I was genuinely surprised that the last of which was unfinished. Tight handwriting, with many crossings-out.

I walked straight ahead, clutching the manuscript under my arm. I was afraid of losing it. A late summer afternoon. I followed rue de la Convention towards the black façade and fences of the Boucicaut hospital.

When I awoke, I realised that the post office where I'd gone to collect the parcel in my dream was the same one where I often used to accompany Dannie. She got her post there. I had asked her why she had her mail sent to poste restante at rue de la Convention. She explained that she had once lived in this neighbourhood and that, since that time, she'd had "no permanent address".

She didn't receive much post. A single letter each time. We would stop in a café down the street, at the corner of rue de la Convention and avenue Félix-Faure, just opposite the metro entrance. She would open the letter and read it in front of me. And then she shoved it in the pocket of her coat. The first time we were in that café, she told me it was a relative writing from the provinces.

She seemed sorry not to live in the neighbourhood any-more. From what I thought I understood – but sometimes she contradicted herself, and didn't really seem to have much sense of what they call chronology – it was the first place she had lived in Paris. Not for long. A few months. I immediately sensed a certain reticence in telling me exactly which province, which region, she came from. One day, she'd said, "When I arrived in Paris at the gare de Lyon . . ." and that sentence must have struck me because I recorded it in my black notebook. It was rare for her to give me such precise details about herself. It was on an evening when we had gone to fetch her post at rue de la Convention, much later than usual. By the time we arrived at the post office, evening had already fallen and it was almost closing time. We had ended up at the café. The waiter, who must have known her since she'd lived in the neighbourhood, served her, without being asked, a glass of Cointreau. She had read the letter and stuffed it in her pocket.

"When I arrived in Paris at the gare de Lyon . . ." The day of her arrival, she told me, she had taken the metro. After several transfers, she had got off here, at Boucicaut station. And she nodded at the metro entrance outside the café window. More-over, she had made the wrong change at one point and found herself at Michel-Ange-Auteuil. I let her talk, knowing how she eluded questions that were too specific: she changed subject, as if she hadn't heard, her mind seemingly elsewhere. Still, I asked her, "Wasn't there anybody to meet you at the gare de Lyon that

Once at the Seine, we didn't take the metro at Javel station, as we normally did to go to the Right Bank. Instead, we turned around and headed back down rue de la Convention. She was intent on showing me the building where she'd lived. When we reached the café, we turned onto avenue Félix-Faure, taking the right-hand pavement. As we approached the building, she said, "I'm going to show you the flat . . . I've kept the key." She had no doubt planned this visit, as she was carrying the key with her. She also said, after darting a glance at the black window of the concierge's lodge: "The concierge always goes out for a bit at this time of day, but try not to make any noise on the stairs." She didn't turn on the hall light. We made our way in the dull glimmer of a nightlight on the ground floor. She leaned on my arm. We walked up pressed against each other, and I thought of an expression that made me want to laugh: "Pussyfooting". She opened the door in the dark, then shut it gently behind us. She felt around for the light switch, and a yellowish glow fell from the ceiling in the vestibule. She cautioned me to speak only in a whisper and not turn on any other lights. Immediately to the right, the half-open door to a bedroom that she said was hers. She pulled me into the hallway in front of us, scarcely brightened by the overhead light in the vestibule. To the left was a room with a table and sideboard. The dining room? To the right was the "living room", judging from the couch and the small glass-door cabinet containing ivory figurines. Since the curtains were drawn, she switched on a lamp on a side table. It gave the same yellowish, muted glow as the ceiling light. To the back, a bedroom containing a large brass bed and wallpaper with sky-blue patterns. A few books were piled on one of the bed-side tables. I was suddenly afraid of hearing the entry door slam and the person who lived there catching us. She opened the drawers of the night tables one by one and rummaged through them. From each, she pulled out a few papers that she shoved into the pocket of her coat. And I remained standing, stiff, watching her, expecting the door to slam at any moment. She opened one glass door of the cabinet facing the bed, but its shelves were empty. She closed it. "Aren't you afraid someone might come?" I murmured. She shrugged. She scanned the titles of the books on the bedside table. She took one, with a red cover, and slid that into her coat pocket as well. She must have known the person who lived there, since the lock on the door hadn't changed. She switched off the bedside light and we left the room. At the other end, the yellowish glow from the ceiling and the living-room lamp accentuated the old-fashioned look of the place, with its dark wood sideboard, its ivory figurines in their display case, the worn carpets. "You know the her a Cointreau, and I wondered if it was wise to let ourselves be noticed here after our clandestine visit to the flat. I had hidden the carrier bag under the table. She pulled the book and papers from the pocket of her coat. Later, she told me she was glad to have retrieved that book, a cherished possession that someone had given her as a child. She had almost lost it several times, and each time she found it again, like those faithful objects that refuse to abandon you. It was a French edition of *Rupert of Hentzau* by Anthony Hope, an old copy with a damaged red cover. Among the papers she was examining, several letters, an expired passport, some calling cards ... It was almost nine p.m., but the waiter and the man who was his boss, on the telephone over behind the bar, seemed to have forgotten our presence. "We left the light on in the living room," she suddenly blurted. More than anxiety, the realisation caused her a certain sadness or regret, as if the banal act of going back to turn off the light was denied her. "I knew I'd forgotten something ... I should have checked the wardrobe in my room to see if there were any clothes left ..." I offered to go back up to the flat to turn off the living-room light and fetch her clothes, if she'd lend me the key. Or perhaps I didn't need the key – I could simply knock on the door. The person who lived in the flat, if he was back, would open, and I would say that I'd come on her behalf. I proposed this as if it were the most natural thing in the world, hoping she'd tell me more. I had come to understand that you couldn't ask her a direct question. "No, no, it's out of the question," she said in a calm voice. "They must think I'm dead . . ." "Dead?" "Yes . . . or gone, anyway . . ." She smiled at me to mitigate the seriousness in her voice. I pointed out that, in any case, "they" would notice someone had lit the lamp in the living room, and taken the papers, the book, the record player and records . . . She shrugged. "They'll think it was a ghost." She gave a brief laugh. After the hesitation and sadness that I'd been surprised to see in her, she now appeared relaxed. "She's an old woman I rented a room from," she said. "And she probably couldn't understand how I could just leave from one day to the next, without a word. But I'd rather make a clean break. I don't like goodbyes." I wondered if that was the truth or if she was trying to mollify me and avoid further questions. Why, if it was an "old woman", had she initially said "they"? No matter. There, in that café, I didn't really feel the need to ask her any questions. Rather than always subjecting others to inter-rogations, it's better to accept them as they are, without comment. Besides, I might have had a vague premonition that I would be asking myself those same questions later on. And in fact, three or four years later, I was in a car one evening at the

Rond-Point Mirabeau and I saw rue de la Convention stretching in front of me. I had the illusion that if I just stepped out of the car, left it there in the middle of the stalled traffic and started down that street on foot, I would finally be in the open air, weightless. I would trip effortlessly down the right-hand pavement. On the way, I would light a candle in the church of Saint-Christophe-de-Javel. And a little further on, I would find myself between the café and the metro entrance. The waiter wouldn't be sur-prised to see me and, without my even asking, he'd bring me two Cointreaus, setting the glasses side by side. I would ring at the door of the flat to retrieve her clothes. The problem was that I didn't know the exact address of the building, and the façades and entrances in that part of avenue Félix-Faure looked too much alike for me to recognise the right one. That same evening, I thought I heard her slightly husky voice telling me: "An old woman I rented a room from," and that voice sounded so near . . . An old woman . . . I consulted the street directory to try to find the address. I remembered walking past a hotel and a large display window, in which I was surprised to see rows of telephones gleaming in the twilight. One afternoon when she'd gone to get her post, she had arranged to meet me in the café and I strolled along avenue Félix-Faure, towards the building where we had entered like thieves a few evenings before.

interesting . . ." The prospect of returning to her room in Montparnasse didn't seem to appeal. It was that evening, in the metro, that she alluded for the first time to a country house where we might go, but I mustn't mention it to the others. The others were Aghamouri and his crowd: Duwelz, Marciano, Chastagnier . . . I asked her if Aghamouri knew she'd lived in the flat on avenue Félix-Faure. No, he had no idea. She hadn't met him until afterwards, at the Cité Universitaire. And he also had no knowledge of that country house she'd just mentioned to me. A country house about sixty miles from Paris, she had said. No, neither Aghamouri nor anyone else had ever gone with her to the post office where she picked up her mail. "So, I'm the only one who knows your secrets?" I said. We walked down the endless corridor of the Montparnasse metro station and were the only people on the moving walkway. She took my arm and leaned her head on my shoulder. "I hope you know how to keep secrets." We walked along the boulevard as far as the Dôme, then veered off and skirted the walls of the cemetery. She was trying to buy time to keep from running into Aghamouri and the others in the hotel foyer. It was especially Aghamouri she wanted to avoid. I was about to ask her why she felt accountable to him, but on second thoughts it seemed pointless. I believe that already, back then, I had understood that no-one ever answers questions. "We'll have to wait for them to turn out the lights in the foyer before we go in," I said in a vaguely casual tone. "Like before, to get into the flat . . . But the night porter might see us . . ." The closer we came to the hotel, the more I sensed her apprehension. Let there be no-one in the foyer, I thought. She ended up communicating her unease to me. I could already hear Paul Chastagnier saying in his metallic voice, "So what are you lugging around in that bag?" She paused when we reached the street the hotel was on. It was nearly eleven o'clock. "Shall we wait a little longer?" she said. We sat on a bench on the central reservation of boulevard Edgar-Quinet. I had set the carrier bag down next to me. "It was really stupid to leave the light on before in the living room," she said. I was surprised that she was attaching so much importance to it. But now, after all these years, I understand the sadness that had suddenly clouded her features. I, too, experience a strange sensation at the thought of those lamps we forgot to turn off in places to which we never returned . . . It wasn't our fault. Each time, we had to leave fast, on tiptoe. I'm sure that in the country house, too, we left a light on somewhere. And what if I were solely responsible for that negligence or oversight? Today, I'm convinced that it was neither oversight nor negligence, but that at the moment of leaving it was I who you had a sudden sensation of cold, as if his veins were filled with refrigerant. We walked towards them, and I heard Paul Chastagnier's metallic voice:

"So, you been out shopping?"

And he stared at the carrier bag I was holding in my left hand.

"Yes . . . Yes . . . We've been out shopping," Dannie said in a very gentle tone. She was probably trying to bolster her courage. Her composure astounded me, given how worried she'd been only moments before, as we approached the hotel. The one called "Georges" pondered the two of us with his moonlike face and pale skin, so pale he seemed to be wearing pancake make-up. He raised his eyebrows in an expression of curiosity and distrust that I had noticed on him every time he faced someone. Perhaps he was the one Dannie was afraid of. The first time I'd met him in that foyer, she had introduced him: "Georges". He had remained silent and had merely raised his eyebrows. Georges: the sound of that name suddenly took on a disturbing, cavernous quality that matched his face. When we'd left the hotel, Dannie had said to me, "I hear that fellow is dangerous," but she hadn't explained in what way. Did she even know? According to her, he was someone Aghamouri had met in Morocco. She had smiled and shrugged: "Oh, you know, best not to get mixed up in all that . . ."

"Won't you join us for a drink?" Paul Chastagnier offered.

"It's kind of late," said Dannie, still in that gentle voice.

Aghamouri, who hadn't risen from the armrest of Gérard Marciano's chair, stared at the two of us in astonishment. It seemed to me his face had gone pale.

"Too bad you can't stay a little while. You could have told us all about your shopping adventures."

This time, Paul Chastagnier was speaking directly to me. Clearly, the carrier bag aroused his curiosity.

"Will you help me bring these things up to my room?" She had turned to me, suddenly using the formal *vous* and pointing at the bag. It was as if she were expressly drawing their attention to it, rubbing it in.

I followed her towards the lift, but instead she took the stairs. She went up ahead of me. On the first-floor landing, when they could no longer see us, she moved closer and murmured in my ear:

"It's better if you leave. Otherwise I'm going to have trouble with Aghamouri."

I walked her to her room. She took the carrier bag from me. She said under her breath, as if they might hear:

"Tomorrow at noon at the Chat Blanc."

That was a rather dreary café on rue d'Odessa, with a back

seated with the others. It was just postponing the inevitable, I told myself. Tomorrow he'd ask about me and Dannie, and the prospect filled me with dread. I had nothing to tell him. Nothing. And besides, I've never known how to answer questions.

Outside, I couldn't help looking back at them through the window. And today, as I write this, I feel as if I'm still watching them, standing on that pavement, as if I'd never left it. Still, however much I look at "Georges", the one she said was "dangerous", I no longer feel the disquiet that sometimes used to grip me when I mingled with those people in the foyer of the Unic Hôtel. Paul Chastagnier, Duwelz and Gérard Marciano lean in towards "Georges" for all eternity, planning what Aghamouri called "their dirty tricks". It will end badly for them, in prison, or some obscure vendetta. Aghamouri, sitting on the armrest, keeps silent, observing them with anxious eyes. He was the one who had told me, "Watch out. They can drag you down a very bad path. My advice is to break off relations while there's still time." Soon after that evening, he arranged to meet me at the entrance to the Censier branch of the university. He was eager to "clear the air". I had thought he wanted to scare me off from seeing Dannie again. And now he, too, is behind that window for all eternity, his anxious eyes fixed on the others as they conspire in low voices. And I feel like telling him, in turn, "Watch out." Personally, I was in no danger. But I wasn't fully aware of that at the time. It took me several years to realise it. If I remember correctly, I nonetheless had a vague premonition that none of them would ever drag me down a "very bad path". Langlais, questioning me at the quai de Gesvres, had said, "You really used to keep some mighty peculiar company." He was mistaken. All those people I met, I saw only from a great distance. That night, I don't know how long I remained in front of the hotel window, watching them. At a certain moment, Aghamouri stood up and walked towards the window. He would surely notice that I was there on the pavement. I didn't budge an inch. Too bad if he came outside and joined me. But his eyes were elsewhere and he didn't see me. The one called "Georges" stood up in turn and went with his heavy gait to stand next to Aghamouri. They were only a few centimetres away from me behind the window, and the second one, with his moonlike face and hard eyes, didn't notice me either. Perhaps the glass was opaque from inside, like a one-way mirror. Or else, very simply, dozens and dozens of years stood between us: they remained frozen in the past, in the middle of that hotel foyer, and we no longer lived, they and I, in the same space of time.

I WROTE DOWN VERY FEW APPOINTMENTS IN THAT black notebook. Each time, I was afraid that the person wouldn't show up if I committed the date and time of our meeting to paper in advance. One should not be so certain of the future. As Paul Chastagnier said, I "kept a low profile". I felt as if I were living a clandestine existence, and so, in this type of life, one avoids leaving traces or setting down one's comings and goings in black and white. And yet, in the middle of one page of the notebook, I read: "Tuesday. Aghamouri. 7 p.m. Censier." I attached no importance to that meeting, and it didn't bother me to have it spelled out in black letters on the white sheet.

It must have been two or three days after the night when we had arrived late at the Unic Hôtel and I'd been carrying the bag. I was surprised to receive a note from Aghamouri at 28 rue de l'Aude, where I was renting a room. Where had he got my address? From Dannie? I brought him to rue de l'Aude several times, but I think that was much later. My recollections are hazy. Aghamouri had written in his letter: "Don't tell anyone about this meeting. Especially not Dannie. It's strictly between us. You'll understand why." That "you'll understand why" had worried me.

It was already dark. While waiting, I walked around the wasteland in front of the new university building. That evening I had brought along my black notebook, and to pass the time I jotted down the fading inscriptions that still clung to a few buildings and warehouses slated for demolition that bordered the empty lot. I read:

Sommet Brothers – Leathers and Pelts
B. Blumet & Son – Forwarding Agents for Leathers and Pelts
Beaugency Tanneries
A. Martin & Co. – Rawhide
Salting and Tanning – Paris Leather Exchange

As I wrote down those names, I began to feel queasy. I think it shows in my handwriting, which is choppy, almost illegible by the end. Later I added in pencil, in a steadier hand:

It was an obsession of mine to want to know what had occupied a given location in Paris, over successive layers of time. That evening, I thought I could smell the nauseating odour of pelts and rawhide. The title of a documentary came to mind, one that I'd seen when I was too young and that had marked me for life: "The Blood of Beasts". They slaughtered animals in Vaugirard and La Villette, then brought their skins here to be sold. Thousands upon thousands of anonymous beasts. And of all of that, there remained only this waste ground and, for just a little while longer, the names of a few vultures and murderers painted on those half-crumbled walls. And that evening, I had written them down in my notebook. What was the use? I would much rather have known the names of those hundred maidens from the hospital that used to stretch over this plot of land well before the days of the leather exchange.

"You're pale as a ghost . . . Is something the matter?"

Aghamouri was standing in front of me. I hadn't seen him come out of the university building. He was wearing his camel coat and carrying a black briefcase. I was still absorbed in my notes. He said with an embarrassed smile:

"You do recognise me, don't you?"

I was about to show him the names I had just taken down, but back then I always felt people became suspicious if they realised you were writing something, standing over there by yourself. No doubt they were afraid you were stealing something from them, their words, fragments of their life.

"Was your class interesting?"

I had never been to university and I imagined him in a classroom like in primary school, lifting his desktop to take out his grammar and notebook and dipping his nib in the inkwell.

We walked across the empty lot, avoiding the puddles. His camel coat and black briefcase only reinforced my opinion: he couldn't be a student. He looked like someone heading towards a business appointment in a hotel foyer in Geneva. I'd thought we would go as usual to the café on place Monge, but we took the opposite direction, towards the Jardin des Plantes.

"You don't mind if we have a quiet chat while we walk, do you?"

He spoke in a casual, friendly tone, but I could sense some awkwardness, as if he were searching for the right words and expected to find himself on foreign ground where he would not meet anyone he knew. And, in fact, rue Cuvier stretched before us, deserted and silent all the way to the Seine.

"I wanted to warn you . . ."

He had said these words with great seriousness. Then, nothing. Perhaps, at the last minute, he no longer dared continue.

"Warn me about what?"

I had asked the question too bluntly. While I kept a "low profile", as Paul Chastagnier said, I had never followed others' advice. Never. And every time they were surprised – and disappointed – because I had listened so attentively, wide-eyed like a good pupil or pleasant young man. We walked past the low houses that bordered the Jardin des Plantes. I think it was the part of the botanical gardens that contained the zoo. The street was very dimly lit, and at the end of the darkness and silence I was afraid we would suddenly hear the roars of roaming beasts.

"I should have said something earlier . . . It's about Dannie . . ."

I turned to look at him, but he was facing resolutely forward. I wondered if he wasn't deliberately avoiding my eyes.

"I met Dannie at the Cité Universitaire . . . She was looking for someone to lend her a room, and even a student ID . . ."

He spoke slowly, as if trying with every word to inject as much clarity as possible into a very muddled topic.

"I always suspected someone had told her to look me up . . . Otherwise, she never would have thought of coming to the Cité Universitaire . . ."

I, too, had often wondered how a girl like Dannie would know about the Cité. I had asked her one evening when we'd gone to the post office. "You know," she had answered, "I did come to Paris to study." Yes, but study what?

"Through a friend in the Moroccan Pavilion, I was able to get her a student ID and residence card . . . In my wife's name . . ."

Why in his wife's name? He had stopped walking.

"She was afraid to use her own ID . . . When I had to leave the Cité Universitaire, she didn't want to stay there. I introduced her to the others at the hotel in Montparnasse . . . I think they helped her get false papers . . ."

He gripped my arm and pulled me to the opposite pavement. I was surprised by his abrupt desire to cross the street. We had stopped in front of a small building, and perhaps he was afraid someone might overhear us through the windows. On the other side, no such danger. We skirted the gates of the Central Wine Market, bathed in shadow and even more deserted and silent than the street.

"And why," I asked, "did she need false papers?"

It felt like a dream. This often happened in that period of my life, especially after nightfall. Exhaustion? Or that strange, overpowering sensation of déjà-vu, also due to lack of sleep?

Everything gets jumbled in your mind, past, present and future; everything is superimposed. And still today, rue Cuvier strikes me as detached from Paris, in some unknown provincial town, and I can hardly believe that the man walking next to me ever really existed. I still hear my voice in a distant echo: "Why did she need false papers?"

"But her name really *is* Dannie, isn't it?" I asked Aghamouri in a falsely casual tone, dreading what he might reveal.

"Yes, probably . . ." he said curtly. "On her new ID card, I'm not sure. It's not really important . . . On the card I gave her at the Cité Universitaire, she has my wife's name . . . Michèle Aghamouri."

I asked him a question that I regretted the moment I'd said it:

"And what about your wife – does she know about all this?"

"No."

He again became what he had been a few moments earlier, the person I still remember very clearly: a worried man, eternally on the alert.

"This stays between us, alright?"

"You know," I said to him, "I've known how to keep my mouth shut since I was little."

The solemn tone in which I'd spoken those words surprised even me.

"She's done something pretty serious and they might hold her accountable," he blurted out. "That's why she wanted new ID papers."

"Pretty serious? Like what?"

"Ask her yourself. The problem is, if you do ask her, she'll know you heard it from me ..."

A gate was half-open, allowing access to the Central Wine Market, and Aghamouri had stopped in front of it.

"We can cut through here," he said. "I know a café on rue Jussieu. Aren't you tired of walking?"

I passed through the gateway behind him and entered a large courtyard surrounded by half-demolished buildings, like the ones in the former leather exchange. And the same semidarkness as over the empty lot where I had waited not long before . . . Up ahead, a street lamp shed a white light on the still-intact warehouses, whose walls bore painted signs like the ones I had noted in the ruins of the leather exchange.

I turned towards Aghamouri.

"May I?"

I pulled my black notebook from my jacket pocket, and

today I again read the notes I rapidly took down that evening as we walked towards rue Jussieu:

> *Marie Brizard & Roger*
> *Butte de la Gironde*
> *Fine Wines of Algeria*
> *La Loire Warehouses*
> *Libaud, Margerand & Blonde*
> *Brandies and Liqueurs. La Roseraie Cellars . . .*

"Do you do this often?" Aghamouri asked.

He seemed disappointed, as if he feared that everything he had just confided didn't really interest me and my mind was on something else. But there's nothing I can do about it: I was as susceptible back then as I am now to people and things that are about to disappear. We came to a modern building with a brightly lit vestibule, which bore on its façade the inscription "Faculty of Sciences".

We walked through the vestibule, and then through another patch of waste ground up to rue Jussieu.

"Here it is," said Aghamouri.

And he pointed out a café across the street, next to the Lutèce Theatre. People were clustered on the pavement, waiting for the show to begin.

We sat in a corner near the bar. Facing us, on the opposite side of the room, was a row of tables with a few diners.

Now it was my turn to take the initiative and get him to talk. Otherwise, he might start having second thoughts.

"Before, you said Dannie had done something serious . . . I'd really like to know more."

He paused for a moment.

"She's liable to find herself in deep trouble, of a legal nature . . ."

He was searching for the right words – precise, professional terms, the words of a lawyer or policeman.

"She's fairly safe for now . . . But they could find out she was involved in a nasty incident . . ."

"What kind of 'nasty incident'?"

"You'll have to ask her that yourself."

There was a moment of silence between us. An awkward moment. I heard them ringing up the curtain in the theatre next door, announcing the start of the play. Lord, how I would have loved to be in the auditorium with her that evening, among the spectators, and for her not to be involved "in a nasty incident" . . . I couldn't understand Aghamouri's resistance to telling me what that "nasty incident" was.

"My sense is you and Dannie are fairly intimate," I said. He gave me an embarrassed look. "I saw you together one evening, very late, at 'the 66' . . ."

He didn't seem to know what "the 66" was. I explained that it was the café towards the upper end of boulevard Saint-Michel, near the Luxembourg station.

"It's possible . . . We used to go there when we still lived at the Cité Universitaire . . ."

He smiled, as if trying to steer the conversation on to more neutral territory, but I wanted him to keep to the essentials. After all, it was he who had asked to meet. I was carrying his letter, its envelope bearing my name and address, 28 rue de l'Aude. I had slipped it between the pages of my black notebook. Moreover, I still have it; I reread it earlier today, before faithfully copying down its contents on a sheet of the Clairefontaine stationery I've been using for the past few days.

"Don't you think you should let your wife know Dannie is carrying identity papers in her name . . . ?"

I could feel him "crack", and never had that slang term seemed so appropriate. When I think back to that moment, I can even see a network of tiny fissures on the skin of his face. He seemed so worried that I felt like reassuring him. No, none of it was important.

"If you could get back that card I gave her with my wife's name, it would be a huge help . . ."

He knew I wasn't a bad sort. After all, the two or three times we had seen each other, in the evening after his courses at Censier, we would talk about literature. He was fairly knowledgeable about Baudelaire, and had even asked to read my notes about Jeanne Duval.

"Anyway," he said, "the others made her false papers, so she doesn't need that card anymore . . . But be sure not to mention I told you about it . . ."

He looked so distressed that I resolved to do him this favour, without really knowing how. I had qualms about simply rummaging through Dannie's handbag. At first, when I would go with her to the post office, she used to hand the clerk behind the window some kind of identity card. Was it in the name of Michèle Aghamouri? Was that the name on the false papers she had got from the gang at the Unic Hôtel? And which of them, precisely, had done her that favour? Paul Chastagnier? Duwelz? Gérard Marciano? Personally, my money was on "Georges", the man with the moon face and refrigerant in his veins, who was older than the others and inspired fear in them – the one about whom Paul Chastagnier had said, in response to a question of mine: "He's no altar boy, you know . . ."

"I gather you and your wife have a flat near the Maison de la Radio ..."

I was afraid he would think me indiscreet. But instead, he smiled, and I sensed he was relieved to have it out in the open.

"Yes, that's right ... A tiny little place ... We'd like to have you over sometime, my wife and I ... but on condition that you forget I know Dannie, the Unic Hôtel and the others while you're over there ..."

He had said "over there" as if it were some faraway land, a neutral country where one was safe from harm.

"So basically," I said, "you only have to cross the Seine to forget all about what you've left behind."

"Do you really think so?"

I could see he wanted some kind of comfort. I believe he trusted me ... Whenever we were alone, or walking from place Monge to Montparnasse, we talked about literature. It wasn't as if he could do that with the others, the ones from the Unic Hôtel. I had a hard time imagining Paul Chastagnier, or Duwelz or "Georges" taking an interest in the fate of Jeanne Duval. Gérard Marciano, perhaps? One day, he had confided to me that he wanted to try being a painter, and that he knew an "artists' joint" on rue Delambre, the Rosebud. Many years later, in the file that Langlais handed over to me, there was a police report on Marciano with two mug shots, front and profile, and the Rosebud was mentioned as one of his hang-outs.

He raised his eyes to me.

"Unfortunately, I don't think it's enough just to cross the Seine . . ."

Once again he had that timid smile that threatened to fade at any moment.

"Dannie isn't the only one . . . There's me, too, Jean – I've got myself in a hell of a mess . . ."

It was the first time he called me by my first name, and I was touched. I kept quiet so that he'd go on talking. I was afraid that a single word might cut short any further confidences.

"I'm afraid to go home to Morocco . . . It would be the same as Paris . . . Once you've caught a finger in the works, it's very hard to pull your hand out . . ."

What "works" was he talking about? In the gentlest possible voice, almost a whisper, I asked him a question, a shot in the dark:

"When you were living at the Cité Universitaire, didn't you feel safe?"

He knit his brow, giving his face a studious look – no doubt the face he made at the Censier branch to reassure himself he was just a simple student.

"You know, Jean, there was a strange atmosphere in that place, the Cité, the Moroccan Pavilion ... Frequent police checks ... They wanted to keep an eye on the residents, for political reasons. Certain students were opposed to the Moroccan government ... And Morocco asked France to put them under surveillance ... That's all ..."

He seemed relieved to confide in me. Even a bit breathless. That's all. After that preamble, it was surely easier for him to cut to the chase.

"So you might say my position was rather delicate ... I was caught between the two ... I hung out with people on both sides ... You could even say I was playing both sides ... But it's much more complicated than that ... In the end, you can never play both sides ..."

He must have been right, since he confessed it with such gravity ... Curiously, that sentence has lodged in my memory. Over the following years, when I was alone in the street, preferably at night and in certain areas in the west of Paris – one evening near the Maison de la Radio, in fact – I heard Aghamouri's voice saying to me from afar: "In the end, you can never play both sides."

"I wasn't careful enough ... I let myself get mixed up in these plots ... You know, Jean, some of the people who frequent the Unic Hôtel maintain close ties with Morocco . . ."

As the time passed, the noise and number of people at the tables increased. Aghamouri spoke in a murmur, and I couldn't make out everything he said. Yes, the Unic Hôtel was the rendezvous for certain Moroccans and the Frenchmen who were "in business" with them . . . What sort of "business"? That "Georges" with the moon face, the one Paul Chastagnier had said was "no altar boy", owned a hotel in Morocco . . . Paul Chastagnier had spent many years living in Casablanca . . . And Marciano was born there . . . And he, Aghamouri, had found himself among these people because of a Moroccan friend who spent time at the Cité Universitaire, but who actually worked for the embassy, as a "security" adviser . . .

He spoke faster and faster, and it was hard for me to keep up with the flood of details. Perhaps he wanted to free himself of a burden, a secret he had carried too long. He suddenly said:

"Forgive me . . . All this must seem incoherent . . ."

Not at all. I was used to listening to people. And even when I didn't understand a word they were saying, I opened my eyes wide and fixed them with a penetrating stare, which gave them the illusion they were addressing an especially attentive interlocutor. My mind would be elsewhere, but my eyes gazed steadily at them, as if I were drinking up their words. It was

83

different with Aghamouri. He was part of Dannie's entourage; I *wanted* to understand him. And I hoped that he'd let slip a few clues about the "nasty incident" she was "involved in".

"You're lucky ... You don't have to get your hands dirty like we do ... You can keep your hands clean ..."

Those last words contained a hint of reproach. Who did he mean by "us"? He and Dannie? I looked at his hands. They were delicate, much more delicate than mine. And white. Dannie's, too, had impressed me with their refinement. She had very graceful wrists.

"Except, you have to be careful not to mix with the wrong people ... However invulnerable you think you are, there's always a chink in the armour ... Always ... Be careful, Jean ..."

It was as if he envied me for having "clean hands" and was anticipating the moment when I'd finally get them dirty. His voice grew increasingly distant. And, as I write these lines, that voice is as feeble as the ones that reach you very late at night on the radio, buried in static. I believe I already felt that way at the time. It seems to me that back then I saw them all as if they were behind the glass partition of an aquarium, and that glass stood between them and me. So it is that in dreams you watch others live through the uncertainties of the present, while you know the future. You try to persuade Mme du Barry not to return to France to keep her from being guillotined. This evening, I think I'll take the metro to Jussieu. As the stations roll by, I will travel back in time. I'll find Aghamouri sitting at that same spot near the bar, in his camel coat, his black briefcase lying flat on the table – the black briefcase that might or might not have contained his course notes from Censier, which he said would help him pass his "foundation" exams. I wouldn't have been surprised if instead he had pulled out wads of cash, a pistol, or files to pass on to that Moroccan friend from the Cité Universitaire, the one who worked as an "adviser" at the embassy . . . I'll make him come with me to Jussieu station and we'll take the opposite journey, forward in time. We'll get off at Eglise-d'Auteuil, the end of the line. A quiet evening, in a peaceful, almost rustic, square. I'll tell him, "This is the situation. You're in the Paris of today. You no longer have anything to fear. Anyone who posed a threat is long dead. You're out of harm's way. There are no more phone booths. To call me, at any hour of the day or night, you use this thing." And I'll hand him a mobile.

"Yes . . . Be careful, Jean . . . When you were at the Unic Hôtel, I saw you talking a few times with Paul Chastagnier . . . He'll get *you* involved in some sordid business, too . . ."

It was late. People were exiting the Lutèce Theatre. No-one was left at the dining tables facing us. Aghamouri seemed even more anxious than at the beginning of our conversation. I sensed that he was afraid to go outside, that he'd stay in this café until closing time.

I asked him again:

"And what about Dannie?... Do you really think that 'nasty incident' you were talking about..."

He didn't leave me time to finish. He said, sharply:

"It could cost her dearly . . . Even with false papers, they could still find her . . . It was a mistake to bring her to the Unic Hôtel and introduce her to the others . . . but it was just to give her a break . . . She should have left Paris right away..."

He had forgotten my presence. No doubt he repeated the same words to himself when he was alone, at that hour of night. Then he shook his head as if snapping out of a bad dream.

"I mentioned Paul Chastagnier ... But the most dangerous one of all is 'Georges' . . . He provided Dannie with the false papers. He has major backers in Morocco and knows that friend from the embassy . . . They want me to do something for them..."

He was on the verge of telling me everything, but he stopped himself.

"I don't get why a boy like you should hang out with those people . . . I had no choice, but what about you?"

I shrugged.

"You know," I said to him, "I don't hang out with anyone. Most people I couldn't care less about. Except for Restif de La Bretonne, Tristan Corbière, Jeanne Duval and a few others."

"If that's true, you're very lucky . . ."

And, like a detective who pretends to take your side the better to extort a confession:

"When you get down to it, all this is really Dannie's fault, don't you think? If you want my advice, steer clear of that girl . . ."

"I never take advice."

I forced myself to smile at him, a guileless smile.

"Watch out for yourself . . . Dannie and I, it's as if we had the plague . . . Around us, you're in danger of catching leprosy . . ."

What he was trying to tell me was that there was a tight bond between the two of them, common ground, complicity.

"Don't worry too much about me," I said.

When we left the café, it was nearly midnight. He stood

very stiff in his camel coat, black briefcase hanging from his hand.

"Forgive me . . . I kind of lost my head tonight . . . Don't pay any attention to what I said . . . It must be because of my exams. I never get much sleep . . . I have to take an oral in a few days . . ."

He had recovered all his scholarly dignity and gravitas.

"I don't do nearly as well in oral exams as in written."

He forced himself to smile. I offered to accompany him to the Jussieu metro stop.

"What an idiot I am . . . I didn't even think to offer you dinner."

He was no longer the same man. He had completely regained his self-possession.

We walked calmly across the square. We still had time before the last metro.

"You mustn't take any notice of what I said about Dannie . . . It's not as serious as all that . . . And anyway, when you're fond of someone, you take their concerns way too personally and worry for no reason . . ."

He said this in a clear voice, emphasising every word. An expression occurred to me: he's muddying the waters.

He was about to go down the steps of the metro entrance.

I couldn't keep from asking:

"Are you sleeping at the Unic Hôtel tonight?"

He was not expecting the question. He paused for a moment.

"I don't think so . . . I took back my old room at the Cité Universitaire . . . It's more pleasant, all in all . . ."

He shook my hand goodbye. He was in a hurry to leave, since he went down the steps very fast. Before diving into the corridor, he looked back, as if afraid that I'd run after him. And I was tempted to do it. I imagined we were sitting side by side on one of those dark-red benches on the platform, waiting for a train that would take a long time to arrive because of the late hour. He had lied to me: he was not going back to the Cité Universitaire, or he would have taken the Porte d'Italie line. He was going back to the Unic Hôtel. He would get off at Duroc. Once again, I tried to find out what "nasty incident" Dannie had drifted into. But he didn't answer. There, on the bench, he pretended not to know me. He stepped into the metro car, the doors closed behind him, and, his forehead pressed against the glass, he stared at me with dead eyes.

THAT NIGHT, I RETURNED TO RUE DE L'AUDE ON FOOT.
The long walk encouraged me to lose myself in my thoughts.
On nights when Dannie joined me in my room, it was often
around one in the morning. Sometimes she would say, "I went
to see my brother," or, "I was at my girlfriend's in Ranelagh,"
without offering many details. From what I had gathered, this
brother – sometimes she referred to him as "Pierre" – did not
live in Paris but came to town regularly. And the "girlfriend
in Ranelagh" was so called because her home was near the
Ranelagh gardens, in the sixteenth arrondissement. While
she never offered to let me meet her brother, she did say she
would introduce me someday to her "girlfriend in Ranelagh".
But the days went by and her promise remained unkept.

Perhaps Aghamouri had not lied to me; perhaps, as I walked
towards rue de l'Aude, he was already back in his room at the

Cité Universitaire. But Dannie? I could still hear Aghamouri's voice, like a fading echo: "She's done something pretty serious . . . She's liable to find herself in real trouble . . ." And I was afraid I would be waiting for her in vain that night. Then again, I often waited without knowing if she'd show. Or else, she would come by when I wasn't expecting her, at around four in the morning. I would have fallen into a light sleep, and the sound of the key turning in the lock would startle me awake. Evenings were long when I stayed in the neighbourhood to wait for her, but it seemed normal to me. I felt sorry for people who had to jot down appointments in their diary, some-times months in advance. Everything was prearranged for them, and they would never wait for anyone. They would never know how time throbs, dilates, then falls slack again; how it gradually gives you that feeling of holidays and infinity that others seek in drugs, but that I found just in waiting. Deep down, I felt sure you would come sooner or later. At around eight in the evening, I heard my neighbour shut her door, her steps growing fainter down the stairs. She lived one flight up. On her door was a small, white square of cardboard on which she had written her first name in red ink: Kim. She was about the same age as us. She was performing in a play and had told me she was terrified of arriving late, after the curtain went

escape the sense of emptiness I feel. Taxi waiting at eight in the evening, fear of arriving after the curtain went up, parka against the cold and snow, once-common gestures fallen into disuse, a play that no-one will ever see again, long-gone laughter and applause, the theatre itself demolished . . . We counted for so little in his life . . . On her Mondays off, there was a light in her window, and that, too, reassured me. The other evenings, I was alone in that small building. I sometimes felt I had lost my memory and couldn't understand what I was doing there. Until Dannie returned.

I WAS WALKING WITH HER IN THE NEIGHBOURHOOD where I grew up, an area I normally avoided because it brought back painful memories – an area now so changed that it has become completely foreign and indifferent to me. We went past the Royal Saint-Germain and arrived in front of the Hôtel Taranne. I saw that writer I admired coming out of the hotel, the one who had written a poem called "Dannie". Behind us, a man's voice called out, "Jacques!" and he turned around. He glanced at me in surprise, thinking I'd been the one to call him by name. I was tempted to take advantage of the coincidence, walk up and shake his hand. I would have asked him why his poem was called "Dannie" and whether he, too, had known a girl by that name. But I didn't dare. Someone came up to him, once more saying "Jacques", and he realised his mistake. I think he even smiled at me. The two men followed the boulevard ahead of us, walking towards the Seine.

"You should go say hello to him," Dannie said. She even offered to accost him for me, but I held her back. And then it was too late: they had disappeared, heading left onto boulevard Raspail. We turned back. Once more, we were at the entrance of the Hôtel Taranne.

"Why don't you leave a note for him, asking to meet?" Dannie said.

No – but the next time I ran into him, I would overcome my shyness and go and shake his hand. Unfortunately, I never saw him again, and decades later I learned from a friend of his that if you shook his hand, he would make a weary face and say, "Still only five fingers?" Yes, sometimes life can be monotonous and quotidian, like today when I'm writing these pages, hoping to find an escape route and vanish through a breach in time. The two of us were sitting on the bench between the taxi stand and the Hôtel Taranne. The following year, I would also learn that a crime had been committed on that very spot, just behind us. They had made a man – a Moroccan politician – get into a car, supposedly a police car, but it was actually a kidnapping, then a murder. And the name of that "Georges" who often sat in the foyer of the Unic Hôtel had been cited in the papers as one of the perpetrators. And each time, I expected to find the names of Paul Chastagnier, Duwelz, Gérard Marciano and Aghamouri, whose thoughts about all this I would have loved to know. But it frightened me, and I recalled what he had said that evening in the café near the Lutèce Theatre: "It's as if we had the plague . . . Around us, you're in danger of catching leprosy . . ." One afternoon, I entered a telephone booth at the western edge of town, near Auteuil. And that distance helped reassure me. It felt as if the Unic Hôtel were in another city. I dialled the number of the Moroccan Pavilion at the Cité Universitaire, which Aghamouri had given me the first time I met him with Dannie and which I'd jotted down in my black notebook: POR 58-17. There was little chance he would still have a room there. I heard myself asking in a flat voice: "May I speak to Ghali Aghamouri?"

There was a moment's silence. I nearly hung up. But I was seized by vertigo, like someone who could take cover but instead feels the sudden impulse to run towards danger.

"Who's calling?"

The man had asked the question in the gruff tones of a police inspector.

"A friend."

"I asked for your name."

I was about to succumb to that vertigo, give him my name and address. But I checked myself in time.

"Tristan Corbière."

A pause. He must have been writing it down.

"And why do you want to speak to Ghali Aghamouri?"

"Because I want to speak to him."

I, too, had adopted a gruff tone, even gruffer than his.

"Ghali Aghamouri no longer lives at the Moroccan Pavilion. Did you get that, mister? Did you get that?"

This time I kept silent. And I could feel the person at the other end of the line growing tense, even anxious, because of my silence. I hung up. After that, I often walked on the block where the Royal Saint-Germain and the Hôtel Taranne had been located, but neither one existed anymore, as if they had wanted to alter the crime scene to make people forget. Last week, I even noticed that they'd removed the bench next to the taxi stand where we had sat that evening, Dannie and I.

"It's stupid . . . I could have gone up to him before and told him my name is Dannie, like in his poem . . ."

She laughed. Yes, that man, judging from what I had read of him and from his easy-going looks, would surely have been kind enough to spend a few moments with us. Sometimes, when I walked alone in the street, I would recite verses he had written:

> *If I die then go my bride*
> *To Javel near Citron . . .*

Saint-Christophe-de-Javel. We were in fact coming back from that neighbourhood, where I had accompanied Dannie to the post office, as usual. On the way, I had wanted to tell her everything Aghamouri had said, that "nasty incident" he had alluded to, but I couldn't find the words, or rather the right tone, a light-hearted tone, almost jocular, so as not to scare her away . . . I was afraid she'd get her back up – as they said in certain circles, no doubt including the Unic Hôtel – and that it would create distance between us.

We were about to take rue de Rennes and follow it to Montparnasse. But on the threshold of that wide, sad, rectilinear street that stretched seemingly into infinity – the Tour Montparnasse had not yet darkened it with its funereal block – I recoiled. I asked if she really needed to go back to the Unic Hôtel.

"I have to see Aghamouri," she said, "so he can give me some papers."

It was time to clear the air once and for all. I hesitated a few seconds more. Then:

"What kind of papers? Papers in the name of Michèle Aghamouri?"

She stared at me, dumbfounded, frozen on the pavement, in front of what is now a Monoprix and what was then an abandoned garden plot that sheltered dozens of stray cats.

"Did he tell you that?"

"Yes."

Her expression hardened, and I thought of Aghamouri. If he had been in front of her at that moment, she would have clawed his eyes out. Then she shrugged and said in an indifferent voice:

"I know it seems a little strange, but it's completely normal . . . Michèle lent me her student ID . . . I've lost all my papers and I have to turn handsprings to get a copy of my birth certificate . . . I was born in Casablanca . . ."

Was it just coincidence? She, too, had ties with Morocco.

"He also told me that someone had got you false papers."

I had said "someone" because I didn't really know the name of the man with the moon face the others called "Georges", or whether that was his first name, a pseudonym, or even his family name.

"Oh, no, nothing like that, no false papers . . . Do you mean Rochard? The one who's usually in the hotel foyer?"

"The one they call 'Georges'..."

"That's him," she said. "Rochard . . . He often goes to Morocco ... He has a hotel in Casablanca ... And since I was born there, he was able to get me temporary papers ... While waiting for the real ones to be ready . . ."

We did not take rue de Rennes. Perhaps the thought of heading to Montparnasse down that wide, mournful street and returning to the Unic Hôtel made her apprehensive, too. We walked towards the Seine.

"Aghamouri told me you needed false papers because you'd got involved in a nasty incident . . ."

We had arrived in front of the Ecole des Beaux-Arts. Students were gathered on the pavement, celebrating something. Some were clutching musical instruments; others were dressed up as various characters – musketeers, jailbirds – or were simply bare-chested, with different-coloured stripes painted on their skin like Red Indians.

"He used the words 'nasty incident'?"

She was staring at me, frowning. She seemed not to understand. The others, around us, whooped and played their instruments. I was sorry I had spoken those words: false papers, nasty incident. And to think that we could have been like those nice students who were blocking our path . . . They invited us to come to their gala later that night. The "Bal des Quat'z'Arts". We had a hard time extricating ourselves, but finally their voices and music grew fainter behind us.

"Aghamouri even wanted me to get back the card with his wife's name that he'd given you ..."

She burst out laughing, and I couldn't tell if her laughter was natural or forced.

"And to top it off, he told you I got myself involved in a nasty incident? And you *believed* all that, Jean?"

We walked along the quays, and I was relieved that we were there rather than in dismal, stifling rue de Rennes. At least there was space and I could breathe. And very little traffic. And silence. We could hear the sound of our footsteps.

"He's talking nonsense . . . *He's* the one who got involved in a nasty incident . . . Didn't he tell you?"

"No."

None of this was important. The only thing that mattered was that we were strolling along the quays without asking anyone's permission and without leaving anything behind. And we could just as easily cross over the Seine and lose ourselves in other neighbourhoods, and even leave Paris for other cities and another life.

"They're using him to lure someone into a trap, a Moroccan

who often comes to Paris . . . He's not completely on board, but he got himself caught up in it . . . He can't refuse them anything . . ." I was barely listening to what she said. For me, it was enough to be with her on the quays and hear the sound of her voice. I wasn't really interested in those bit players from the Unic Hôtel: Chastagnier, Marciano, Duwelz, the one they called "Georges" but who called himself Rochard, those individuals whose names I force myself to repeat so that they don't fade from my memory altogether.

"And what about you?" I asked. "Are you obliged to keep seeing those people?"

"Not at all . . . It was Aghamouri who introduced us. I have nothing to do with them."

"Not even with Rochard?"

It had been an effort to ask that question. That Rochard, whom they called "Georges", was no less indifferent to me than the others.

"I just asked him for a small favour . . . That's all . . ."

"And is your name still Dannie on your false papers?"

"Don't make fun of me, Jean . . ."

She had taken my arm, and we crossed over the Pont Royal. I don't know why I always felt a burden lift when I crossed the Seine on that bridge, towards the Right Bank.

In the middle of the bridge, she stopped short and said:

"Whether those papers are real or fake, does it really make any difference to us?"

No. No difference at all. Back then, I wasn't certain of my own identity, so why should she have been any more so? Still today, I have doubts about the authenticity of my birth certificate, and until the very end I'll be waiting for someone to hand me the long-lost document that shows my real name, my real date of birth, the names of the real parents I never knew.

She leaned towards me and whispered in my ear:

"You still ask yourself way too many questions . . ."

I think she was wrong. It's only today, dozens and dozens of years later, that I'm trying to decode the signals that this mysterious correspondent has sent me from the far reaches of the past. At the time, I was content to live day by day, without asking many questions at all. And besides, the ones I asked her – they were few, and not very insistent – she never answered. Except for one evening, between the lines. It was only twenty years later, thanks to the file Langlais had given me, that I learned what "nasty incident" she'd been involved in, as Aghamouri had put it. He had said, "Something serious." It was serious, alright. There had even been a homicide.

Earlier this evening, I was leafing through Langlais's file and again came across one of those onionskin sheets containing these very precise details: "Two projectiles struck the victim. One of the two projectiles was fired point blank. The other was fired neither point blank nor at a short distance . . . The two slugs corresponding to the two spent shells were found . . ." But I don't have the heart to transcribe the rest. I'll come back to it later, someday when the weather is clear and the sun and blue sky dissipate the shadows.

We crossed through the Tuileries. I wonder what season it was. Today, as I write these lines, it seems to me it was in January. I see patches of snow in the Carrousel gardens, and on the pavement where we walked next to the Tuileries. In front of us, the lamp posts under the arcades on rue de Rivoli are shrouded in a halo of fog. Still, I'm not sure: it could be early autumn. The trees in the Tuileries haven't shed their leaves. They will lose them soon, but for me autumn does not evoke the end of something. I believe the new year begins in October. Winter. Autumn. The seasons vary and blend together in retrospect, as if memories, rather than being fixed, dead images, lived a life of their own over the years, like a kind of plant life. Yes, the seasons often blend into each other: spring and winter, Indian summer . . . When we reached the arcades, rain was falling very hard, or maybe it was one of those sudden downpours that catch you in summer.

"Do I really look like someone who'd get involved in a nasty incident?"

She leaned her face near mine, as if she wanted me to examine it closely, and looked me squarely in the eye, with such a frank gaze ...

"If I had got involved in something sordid, I would tell you ..."

I still hear that sentence at night, in hours of insomnia. I had written it down in my black notebook. Still, I must have had my doubts, some vague premonition, to set it down there in black and white. Why didn't she tell me anything? At most she dropped hints, like that evening as we left the gare de Lyon, and at the time I hadn't paid it much attention. Perhaps she was trying not to frighten me off, but if that's the case she didn't know me. I don't remember which moralist I was reading when I lived on rue de l'Aude who said that one must always take the people one loves on their own terms, and especially not demand any explanations from them.

"You know," she said, "pretty soon I'm going to break it off with those losers from the Unic Hôtel."

Normally so refined in her vocabulary and her diction, every once in a while she came out with a slang word, some of which I didn't know and took down in my black notebook: nick, dirt nap, rozzer, flea in his ear. I also found, on a page of the notebook, in parentheses, "those losers from the Unic Hôtel", and I wonder whether I wasn't planning at the time to use it as the title of a novel.

"You're right," I said. "You can always count on the people who write to you at the post office."

I had laced those words with a sarcasm that I immediately regretted. But, after all, she was the one who'd started it, by saying "those losers from the Unic Hôtel" in such a mocking tone.

She suddenly looked sad.

"It's mostly my brother who writes to me at the post office..."

She had said it very fast, in a hoarse voice that I'd never heard before, and there was so much candour in her avowal that I kicked myself for having doubted the existence of a brother she refused to introduce to me.

Post office. Poste restante. In Langlais's file, there was a dirty white sheet of paper that resembled a civil status document. This evening, I examine it again, hoping it will finally divulge her secret: on the poor-quality photobooth image stapled to the left-hand margin, I recognise Dannie with shorter hair.

And yet the form is in the name of one Mireille Sampierry, residing at 23 rue Blanche, Paris 9th. It is dated the year before we met and bears the heading "Certificate of Authorisation to Receive Correspondence and Telegrams Poste Restante without Surcharge". Even then it is not for the post office on rue de la Convention, where I had accompanied her on several occasions, but for "Branch no. 84" at 31 rue Ballu (9th). To how many poste restante addresses did she have her mail sent? How had this form fallen into the hands of Langlais or members of his squad? Had Dannie left it somewhere? And that name, "Mireille Sampierry" – is that the name Langlais had questioned me about in his office on quai de Gesvres? It's funny how certain details of your existence, invisible at the time, are revealed to you twenty years later, as when you look at a familiar photograph through a magnifying glass and a face or object that you hadn't noticed before jumps out at you . . .

She pulled me to the right, under the arcades of rue de Castiglione.

"Let me take you to dinner . . . It's not too far from here . . . We can walk . . ."

At that hour, the area was deserted and the echo of our footsteps rebounded beneath the arcades. Around us reigned the kind of silence that ought to be broken not by a passing car but by the clack of hooves from a carriage horse. I don't know whether I thought this at the time or whether the idea occurred to me just now as I write these lines. We were lost in the nocturnal Paris of Charles Cros and his dog Satin, of Tristan Corbière and even of Jeanne Duval. Traffic flowed around the Opéra, and we were once again in the Paris of the twentieth century, which today seems so far away ... We followed rue de la Chaussée d'Antin, which ended at the dark façade of the church, like a giant bird at rest.

"We're almost there," she said. "It's at the beginning of rue Blanche ..."

Last night, I dreamed that we were following the same route, probably because of what I had just written. I heard her voice: "It's at the beginning of rue Blanche," and I slowly turned towards her. I said:

"At number 23?"

She appeared not to hear. We walked at a steady pace, her arm in mine.

"I once knew a girl named Mireille Sampierry who lived at 23 rue Blanche."

She didn't react. She remained silent as if I hadn't said a word, or as if the distance between us in time was so great that my voice could no longer reach her.

But that evening, I didn't yet know the name Mireille Sampierry. We skirted the square in front of Trinité church.

"You'll see . . . It's a place I really like . . . I used to go there a lot when I lived on rue Blanche . . ."

I remember that, by association, I thought of Baroness Blanche. I had taken notes about her several days earlier, in my notebook, copying a page from a history of Paris under Louis XV: it was a report that summarised the little information we possess about the baroness' chaotic and adventurous life.

"Do you know why the street is named that?" I asked her. "It's because of Baroness Blanche."

A few days before, she had wanted to know what I was writing in my notebook, and I had read her my notes about that woman.

"So I used to live on 'Baroness Blanche Street'?" she said with a smile.

The restaurant was located at the corner of rue Blanche and the small side street that led back to Trinité church. The curtains were drawn behind its front windows. She went in ahead of me, as if entering a familiar place. A large bar at the rear, and on either side a row of round tables with white tablecloths. The walls looked dark red because of the muted light. There were only two diners – a man and a woman – at a table near the bar, behind which stood a dark-haired man of about forty.

"Well, look who's here," he said to Dannie, as if surprised to see her.

She seemed embarrassed. She said to him:

"I've been away from Paris all this time . . ."

He greeted me with a brief nod. She introduced me.

"A friend."

He seated us at a table near the door, perhaps so that we'd be left in peace, away from the other couple. But those two spoke very little, and in low voices.

"It's nice here," she said to me. "I should have brought you here before . . ."

It was the first time I saw her relax. Anywhere else in Paris I had been with her, I always noticed a hint of worry deep in her eyes.

"I used to live a bit further on . . . in a hotel . . . when I left the flat on avenue Félix-Faure . . ."

As I write these lines, I read on the official form: "Mireille Sampierry, residing at 23 rue Blanche, Paris 9th." But number 23 isn't a hotel: I checked. So, why would she tell me she'd lived in a hotel? Why that seemingly innocuous lie? And that name, Mireille Sampierry? It's too late to ask her now, except in my dreams when different time periods merge together and I can ask whatever I want, thanks to what I gleaned from Langlais's file. But there's no point. She cannot hear me, and I experience that strange sensation of absence you feel when you dream about deceased friends and see them so close to you.

"So what have you been up to all this time?"

He was standing near our table. He had served us two glasses of Cointreau, no doubt figuring that we shared the same tastes.

"Trying to find work . . ."

He flashed me a sarcastic look, as if he wasn't taken in by any of this and wanted an ally.

"But she hasn't even introduced us. André Falvet . . ."

He shook my hand, still smiling. I stammered:

"Jean . . ."

I was always embarrassed to introduce myself and enter into someone's life in that abrupt, almost military way, which practically requires you to stand at attention. To keep things less formal, I dispensed with my family name.

"So, did you find any work?"

The sarcasm wasn't only in his look. It was as if he were talking to a child.

"Yes . . . A secretarial job . . . with him . . ."

She pointed to me.

"Secretarial?"

He nodded in false admiration.

"Some people were asking after you. They even asked me a lot of questions, but not to worry, I kept mum . . . I told them you'd gone abroad . . ."

"Well done."

She looked around her, probably to verify that the décor hadn't changed. Then she turned to me:

"It's very peaceful in here . . ."

It felt as if we were removed from everything, in a grotto that no-one else could enter because a heavy red curtain had been drawn over the door. The man and woman at the table to the back had disappeared without my noticing, and now there was no way for me to know who they were.

"Yes, very peaceful," he said to her. "You forgot it's our day off . . ."

He headed back to the bar and, before going through the door that must have led to the kitchen:

"I wasn't expecting anyone for dinner this evening . . . I have to warn you, it'll be pot luck . . ."

She leaned towards me and our foreheads touched. She whispered:

"He's very nice . . . Nothing like those guys at the Unic

Hôtel . . . You can trust him . . ."

I did not understand at the time why she was trying to re-assure me. The man's name, André Falvet, appears in the file that Langlais gave me, and what a strange feeling, every time, when you learn things twenty years after the fact about people you once knew . . . You finally decipher, thanks to a secret code, what you lived through in confusion, without really under-standing . . . A car ride at night with the headlights off, and no matter how tightly you press your forehead against the win-dow, you have no reference points. And besides, did you really ask that many questions about where you were going? Twenty years later, you follow the same path by day and finally see all the details surrounding you. But so what? It's too late, and no-one is left. André Falvet, a member of the Stéfani gang. Served time in Poissy prison. Dog breeder in Porcheville. Manager of Carrol's Beach in La Garoupe. Restaurant La Passée, boulevard Gouvion-Saint-Cyr. Le Sévigné, rue Blanche.

"We should come here more often," she said to me.

We did go back several times. The room was no longer empty, as it had been that first evening. Instead, all the tables were occupied by odd-looking customers, and I wondered if they were locals. Others were seated at the bar, speaking with the aforementioned André Falvet. Some of them are listed in

Langlais's file. Names, mere names, that I'd gladly copy down here, as a shot in the dark, but right now I'm not up to it. I'll do it later, just to be on the safe side. You never know: you should always send out signals. The light was muted, as if the bulbs were of insufficient wattage. Or was the aforementioned Falvet trying to create a more intimate ambience? As I write this, a thought occurs. The light was the same as in the flat on avenue Félix-Faure where she had taken me one evening, and also as in the country house, La Barberie, in Feuilleuse, at dusk. As if the lamps had grown weaker over time. But sometimes, something clicks. Yesterday, I was alone in the street and a veil fell away. No more past, no more present – time stood still. Everything was again in its true light. It was about eight in the evening, in summer, and there was still sunlight at the bottom of rue Blanche. They had placed two or three outdoor tables in front of the restaurant. The door was wide open on the street, and from the dining room one could hear the din of conversation. We were sitting at one of the outdoor tables, Dannie and I. The sun was making us squint.

"I have to show you the hotel where I used to live, a bit further on," she said.

"At number 23?"

"Yes, number 23."

And she did not seem at all surprised that I should know the address.

"But that's not a hotel."

She didn't answer, and it made no difference. She wanted to walk in the neighbourhood before nightfall. But we had plenty of time ahead of us. Thanks to Daylight Saving Time, the sun would still be up at ten o'clock. I even thought it would shine all night.

A SHORT WHILE AGO, I WAS IN A BOOKSTORE ON RUE DE l'Odéon. Night had already fallen. Among the used books, I had discovered a novel in a scuffed red binding whose title was *The Dream Is Over*. The bookseller, at his counter, had just slipped the volume into a white plastic bag and was handing it to me when a woman entered the shop. She hadn't shut the glass door behind her, as if she was in a hurry. A woman my age, a mulatto, tall, wearing an old rust-coloured coat with a hanging belt. She was carrying a large shopping bag. She came up to us and plunked the bag on the counter.

"You buy books?"

She had asked the question abruptly, with an outmoded accent from the old Paris outskirts.

"It depends," said the bookseller.

"An old lady sent me ... I work for her ..."

She yanked the books from the large shopping bag: art books, deluxe volumes from the Pléïade series . . . A necklace and brooch had stuck to one of them, and she shoved them back in the bag. Her movements were staccato, and several banknotes fell out. She scooped them up and thrust them in a pocket of her coat.

"Does this old lady live in the neighbourhood?" asked the bookseller.

"No . . . No . . . She lives in the seventeenth. She's my employer . . ."

"I'll need you to give me her address," said the bookseller.

"What do you need her address for?"

She had suddenly turned aggressive. The necklace, the brooch and the banknotes among the books made it look like a hasty robbery. The books were piled on the counter.

"So, you don't want them?"

"Not right now," said the bookseller.

She threw them back into the shopping bag, furiously, one by one. The bookseller stared at their covers as if looking for bloodstains. Perhaps he figured she had murdered the old lady she called her "employer".

She shrugged and left the shop without shutting the door behind her. Afraid she would vanish, I ran out after her.

The instant I had seen her in the bookstore, I had told myself she was the reincarnation of Jeanne Duval, or perhaps Jeanne Duval in the flesh. Her tall stature, old-style Parisian accent and the large bag in which she stacked the books, jewellery and bank notes corresponded perfectly to the few details I had read about her and had once jotted down in my black notebook. She was walking about ten yards ahead of me and she had a slight limp. I could have caught up with her, but I preferred to follow at a distance to persuade myself it was indeed she. The belt of her coat was hanging down; she was carrying the shopping bag in her left hand, and its weight made her tilt slightly to one side. The lamps on the building façades had not changed since the nineteenth century and barely lit the street. I was afraid I might lose sight of her. At the Carrefour de l'Odéon, she headed towards the metro entrance. I had quickened my step. Just as she was about to descend the stairs, I shouted:

"Jeanne . . ."

She turned around. She threw me a worried glance, as if I had caught her red-handed. For a moment, we remained frozen in place, watching each other. I wanted to go up and accompany her to the station platform, carry her bag for her. I couldn't move. My legs felt like lead, as often happens in my dreams. Then she ran down the stairs. No doubt she was afraid I would follow. She must have taken me for a plainclothesman. In the flush of emotion, I sat down beneath the statue of Danton. She had told the bookseller that her "employer" lived in the seventeenth arrondissement. But of course: it corresponded to the last piece of information I had read about her. It has never been established when she died, and I wondered whether she ever *had* died. Moreover, no-one knew her date of birth. Her shadow still remained very present in certain quarters of Paris. The last witness, who had identified her because he lived nearby, had stated that her address was 17 rue Sauffroy. That was at the far end of the seventeenth arrondissement. A long haul by metro. From Odéon, she would change at Sèvres-Babylone. Then at Saint-Lazare. She would get off at Brochant. I promised myself to go to rue Sauffroy someday. At least I had a vague reference marker. It was more than I could say about the individuals I had known much closer in time than Jeanne Duval, who, like her, were mentioned in my black notebook. I had no idea what had become of them. I believe the ones Dannie called "those losers from the Unic Hôtel" were dead – or at least, "Georges", alias Rochard, was, and Paul Chastagnier. I'm less certain about Duwelz and Gérard Marciano. I never heard from Aghamouri again. And Dannie had vanished for good. Still, on the last page of the black notebook I had made

One winter morning, some twenty years ago, I had been summoned to the courthouse in the thirteenth arrondissement, and at around eleven o'clock, after I left court, I found myself on the pavement of place d'Italie. I had not been back to that square since the spring of 1964, a time when I frequented the area. I suddenly noticed that I didn't have a penny in my pocket for a cab or the metro fare home. I found an A.T.M. in a small side street behind the district town hall, but after I had entered my pin code, a slip of paper came out in lieu of cash. It read: "We're sorry. You have insufficient credit." Again I entered my code, and the same slip of paper came out with the same message: "We're sorry. You have insufficient credit." I skirted the town hall and once again was on the pavement of place d'Italie.

Fate wanted to keep me here and was not to be crossed. Maybe I would never manage to leave this district, since my credit was insufficient. I felt light-hearted because of the sun and blue January sky. The skyscrapers hadn't existed in 1964, but they gradually dissolved in the limpid air to make way for the Clair de Lune café and the squat buildings of boulevard de la Gare. I would slip into a parallel time continuum where no-one could ever reach me.

The paulownias with their mauve flowers in place d'Italie

... I repeated that phrase to myself, and I admit that it brought tears to my eyes – or was it the winter cold? In short, I had returned to my point of departure and, if A.T.M.s had existed in 1964, I would have received the same slip of paper: Insufficient credit. Back then, I had no credit, no legitimacy. No family or defined social status. I floated on the Paris air.

I walked towards the former site of the Clair de Lune. We used to sit for hours at the tables at the back, near the musicians' stand, not ordering anything. I was circling place d'Italie. Perhaps I should take a room in a small hotel, like the Coypel, if it still existed, or another whose name I'd forgotten near Les Gobelins. I arrived at the corner of avenue de la Sœur-Rosalie and again I walked towards the town hall, wondering how long I would keep turning around the square, as if it were a magnetic field holding me in place. I stopped in front of a café. A middle-aged man was seated at a table behind the window, watching me. And I, too, couldn't take my eyes off him. His face reminded me of someone. Regular features. Grey – or white – hair in a long brush cut. He waved to me. He wanted me to come and join him in the café.

He stood at my approach and held out his hand.

"Langlais. Can you place me now?"

I had a moment's hesitation. It was probably his military

stiffness and the "can you place me now" that helped me iden-
tify him. And besides, one never forgets the faces of people one
meets at a difficult time in one's life.

"Quai de Gesvres . . ."

He looked surprised that I should say that.

"You have a good memory . . ."

He sat back down and motioned for me to take the seat
opposite him.

"I've been keeping an eye on you from a distance all this
time," he said. "I even read your last book, the one about that
woman . . . Jeanne Duval . . ."

I didn't quite know what to answer. I repeated:

"You've been keeping an eye on me?"

He smiled, and I recalled that back then he had shown me
some benevolence.

"Yes . . . Keeping an eye . . . It was sort of my job . . ."

He looked at me, knitting his brow, as he had the previous
century in his office on the quai de Gesvres. Apart from his grey
brush cut, he had not changed much. It was not very warm
in that part of the café near the windows and he had kept on
a gaberdine coat that might have dated from the time of my
interrogation.

"I don't suppose you live in this neighbourhood . . . or

I would have seen you before . . ."

"No, I don't live in the neighbourhood," I said. "And I haven't been back here in ages . . . Since the time of quai de Gesvres . . ."

"Will you have something to drink?"

The waiter was standing at our table. I nearly ordered a Cointreau, in memory of Dannie, but I had no money on me and felt embarrassed at being treated.

"Thanks . . . I'm fine," I stammered.

"Oh, go on . . . Order something . . ."

"An espresso."

"Same for me," said Langlais.

There was a moment of silence. It was my turn to break the ice:

"Do *you* live in the neighbourhood?"

"Yes – always have."

"I did, too, when I was younger. I knew this area well . . . Do you remember the Clair de Lune?"

"Of course! But what were you doing at the Clair de Lune?"

His tone was the same as at my interrogation, back then. He smiled.

"You're under no obligation to answer. We're not in my office anymore . . ."

Through the café window, I could see part of place d'Italie that hadn't changed under the sun and blue sky. I felt as if he had questioned me only the day before. I smiled back.

"And where should we pick up the interrogation?" I asked.

He, too, was feeling the same thing, I was sure of it. Time had been erased. Not a day had gone by between the quai de Gesvres and place d'Italie.

"It's funny," he said. "There were several times when I wanted to get in touch with you . . . I even called your publisher once, but they wouldn't give out your address."

He leaned towards me and squinted.

"Mind you, I could have found your address if I wanted . . . It was my job . . ."

He again had the same gruff tone as on the quai de Gesvres. I couldn't tell whether he was joking.

"Only, I didn't want to bother you . . . or give you cause for alarm . . ."

He nodded, looking like he wanted to add something. I waited with folded arms. It was suddenly as if our roles had reversed and *I* was the one behind the desk, about to begin the interrogation.

"So, here's the thing . . . When I retired, I took two or three case files with me, as souvenirs . . . and among them was the file on the people who were the reason why we summoned you to quai de Gesvres ..."

He spoke sheepishly, almost shyly, as if he had just made a compromising admission that might shock me.

"If you're still interested ..."

I wondered if I were dreaming. A man had just sat down at a table near the window at the back, and was punching in a number on his mobile phone. Seeing that object confirmed that it was no dream and that the two of us were here, in the present, in the real world.

"Of course I'm interested," I said.

"That's why I wanted your address ... I thought I'd post you all this ..."

"Odd characters," I said. "I've been thinking about them a lot recently ..."

I wanted to tell him why this case file, which was nearly half a century old, still interested me. You have lived through a short period of your life – day by day, without asking yourself any questions – under strange circumstances, among people who were equally strange. And it's only much later that you can finally understand what you lived through and who those people really were, on condition that someone finally gives you the key to decipher a coded language. Most people aren't in that situation: their memories are simple, straightforward, self-sufficient, and they don't need dozens and dozens of years to clarify them.

"I understand," he said, as if he had read my thoughts. "This file will be a little like a time bomb for you . . ."

He looked over the bill. I was truly embarrassed not to be able to offer to pay. But I didn't dare confess to him that, that morning, my credit was insufficient.

Outside, on the pavement around the square, we were still and silent, Langlais and I. Apparently he didn't want to part company right away.

"I could just hand you the file . . . No need to mail it . . . I live right nearby . . ."

"That would be very kind of you," I said.

We circled place d'Italie, and he pointed to a high-rise on the corner of avenue de Choisy.

"That's where the Clair de Lune used to be," he said, indicating the ground floor. "My father took me there a lot . . . He knew the manageress . . ."

We started up avenue de Choisy.

"I live a bit further on . . . Don't worry, I won't make you walk for miles . . ."

We arrived at square de Choisy. I had a clear recollection

of this public garden, which looked more like a park; of the large red-brick building called the Institut Dentaire, and the girls' school across the way. On the other side of the avenue, after the high-rises, were modest houses of the type I remembered. But how much longer would they be there? Langlais had stopped in front of a small building on the corner of a blind alley, with a Chinese restaurant on the ground floor.

"I won't ask you to come up . . . I'd be too ashamed . . . It's a total pigsty up there . . . I'll just be a moment . . ."

Alone on the pavement, I pondered the leafless trees in square de Choisy and, further on, the dark red mass of the Institut Dentaire. That building had always struck me as an anomaly in this park. My memories of square de Choisy were not memories of winter, but of spring or summer, when the foliage on the trees contrasted with the dark red of the Institute.

"What were you daydreaming about?"

I hadn't heard him come up. In his hand was a yellow plastic folder. He held it out to me.

"Here . . . Your case file . . . It's not very thick, but it might interest you . . ."

We were both reluctant to part company. I would have liked to invite him to lunch.

128

"Please don't take it the wrong way that I didn't ask you up . . . It's a tiny flat that used to belong to my parents . . . Its only plus is the view of all those trees . . ."

He gestured towards the entrance of square de Choisy.

"We were talking about the Clair de Lune before . . . The manageress was murdered over there, in the park. You see . . . That red-brick building . . . the Institute . . ."

He was lost in a painful memory.

"They dragged her over to it . . . They shoved her against the wall and shot her in the back . . . And afterwards, they realised they'd made a mistake . . ."

Had he witnessed the scene from his window?

"It happened after the Liberation of Paris . . . A whole bunch of them had commandeered the building . . . bogus Resistance men . . . Captain Bernard and Captain Manu . . . and a lieutenant whose name I've forgotten . . ."

I hadn't known these details when I used to walk through square de Choisy, years ago, to wait for a childhood friend to come out of the girls' school.

"One shouldn't stir up the past too much. I'm not sure if I did the right thing by giving you that file . . . Did you ever see the girl again? The one with all the aliases?"

At first I didn't understand who he meant.

"The reason why we questioned you. What did you call her?"

"Dannie."

"Her real name was Dominique Roger. But she had other names, too."

Dominique Roger. Perhaps it was under that name that she went to collect her mail at the post office. I had never seen the name on the envelopes. She jammed the letters in her coat pocket immediately after reading them.

"Maybe you knew her as Mireille Sampierry?" asked Langlais.

"No."

He spread open his arms and looked at me with eyes full of compassion.

"Do you think she's still alive?" I asked him.

"Do you really want to know?"

I had never put the question to myself so plainly. If I were being honest, the answer would be, No. Not really.

"What's the point?" he said. "You can't force things. Maybe someday you'll run into her in the street. We found each other, you and I . . ."

I had opened the yellow plastic folder. At a glance, it seemed to contain about ten sheets.

"You'd be better off reading that with a clear head . . . If you have any questions, give me a call."

He fished in his inside jacket pocket and handed me a tiny calling card bearing the words: Langlais, 159 avenue de Choisy, and a telephone number.

After taking a few steps, I turned around. He hadn't gone back inside. He remained standing there, on the pavement, watching me from a distance. He would surely keep his eyes on me until I disappeared at the end of the avenue. Back when he practised his profession, he must have gone on many stake-outs on winter days just like this one, or at night, his hands thrust into the pockets of his gaberdine coat.

"ONE SHOULDN'T STIR UP THE PAST," LANGLAIS HAD SAID as we were parting company, but that winter morning I still had a long walk ahead of me before reaching home at the far end of Paris. Was it really by chance that I'd found myself in place d'Italie after more than twenty years and that the A.T.M. had spat out a slip of paper saying, "We're sorry. You have insufficient credit"? What was there to be sorry about? I was happy that morning, light-hearted. Nothing in my pockets. And that long, steady walk, with occasional rest stops on public benches . . . My only regret was that I didn't have my black notebook. I had made a list of the public benches of Paris over the course of various walks: north–south, east–west – those benches that, each time, marked a pause where one could catch one's breath, and daydream. I no longer saw a very clear distinction between past and present. I had reached Les Gobelins.

Since my youth – and even my childhood – I had done nothing but walk, always in the same streets, to the point where time had become transparent.

I entered the Jardin des Plantes and sat down on a bench in the main alley. Only a few passers-by, owing to the cold. But it was still sunny, and the blue of the sky was my confirmation that time had stood still. I needed only sit there until nightfall and study the sky to discover the few stars I could name, without really knowing if I was correct. And entire passages would come back to mind, from my bedside book at the time of rue de l'Aude: *Eternity by the Stars*. Reading it helped me wait for Dannie. It was as cold back then as it was on this bench in the Jardin des Plantes, and rue de l'Aude was covered in snow. But despite the cold, I leafed through the pages contained in the yellow plastic folder. A letter was appended to them, signed by Langlais, which I hadn't noticed earlier when I had peeked into the yellow folder and he had said to me, "You'd be better off reading that with a clear head." The letter was barely legible, no doubt dashed off in his flat before he came back down to hand me the file.

Dear Sir,
I retired from the Force ten years ago, which means

that I was still working in Vice and Homicide while you were writing many of your books, which I read with unflagging interest.

I naturally remembered your visit to my office on quai de Gesvres, for an interrogation when you were very young. I have a good memory for faces. They often used to kid me about it, saying that even if I'd only seen someone once in the street, I could recognise him from behind ten years later.

When I left the department, I treated myself to a few souvenirs from the old Vice Squad archives, among them the incomplete file on you that I have long wanted to send you. That day has come, thanks to our meeting earlier.

Please be assured of my discretion. Moreover, I believe you wrote somewhere that we live at the mercy of certain silences.

Most cordially yours,

LANGLAIS

PS: To further reassure you: the investigation related to these documents has been definitively closed.

As I leafed through the file, I came across civil status records, reports, interrogation transcripts. Certain names jumped out at me: "Aghamouri, Ghali, Pavillon du Maroc, Cité Universitaire, born June 6, 1938, in Fez. Alleged 'student', attached to the Moroccan security forces. Moroccan Embassy . . . Georges B., alias 'Rochard', medium brown hair, straight nose, prominent bulge. Anyone with further information is asked to notify this department, Turbigo 92-00 . . . Before this court appeared the individual henceforth named Duwelz, Pierre. Seen and approved by the accused . . . Chastagnier, Paul Emmanuel. Height 1m 80. Drives automobile Lancia no. 1934 GD 75 . . . Marciano, Gérard. Distinguishing marks: scar 2 cm in length beside left eyebrow . . ." I flipped through the pages quickly, trying not to linger on any one sheet in particular and each time fearing I would discover a new detail or record about Dannie. "Dominique Roger, alias 'Dannie'. Under the name Mireille Sampierry (23 rue Blanche), alias Michèle Aghamouri, alias Jeannine de Chillaud . . . According to Davin's information, resides at the Unic Hôtel under the name Jeannine de Chillaud, born in Casablanca on . . . She had her mail sent to a poste restante address, as attested by the attached registration form issued by P. O. Branch 84, Paris."

And at the bottom of the pages held together by a paperclip:

"Two projectiles struck the victim. One of the two project-iles was fired point blank ... The two slugs corresponding to the two spent shells were found. The concierge at 46-bis quai Henri-IV ..."

One evening, we had got off a train, Dannie and I, at the gare de Lyon. I think we were returning from that country house called La Barberie. We didn't have any luggage. The station was packed. It was summer and, if I remember correctly, the start of the holidays. We left the railway station without taking the metro. She didn't want to return to the Unic Hôtel that evening, so we decided to walk to my place on rue de l'Aude. As we were about to cross the Seine, she said:

"Would you mind if we make a small detour?"

She led me along the quays towards the Ile Saint-Louis. Paris was deserted, as it often is on evenings in summer, and it marked a contrast with the crowds in the gare de Lyon. Very little traffic. A feeling of lightness, of vacation. I had written that last word in capitals in my black notebook, with a date: July 1, the date of that evening. I had even added a definition of "vacation" that I'd seen in a dictionary: "An act or instance of leaving or nullifying; a time of respite."

We followed the quai Henri-IV, which in fact is mentioned at the bottom of that page in Langlais's file, a page on which it is clearly specified that a "homicide" had taken place. She stopped at one of the last addresses, number 46-bis, the same address as on the page – I verified it the day I met Langlais, twenty years later. That day, I merely had to cross the bridge from the Jardin des Plantes.

She headed towards the carriage entrance, then paused for a moment:

"Would you do me a favour?"

Her voice sounded shaky, as if she found herself in a danger zone where she could be caught unawares.

"Ring at the door on the ground floor and ask for Mme Dorme."

She looked at the ground-floor windows, their closed metal shutters. A dim glow filtered through the slits.

"Do you see a light on?" she asked in a whisper.

"Yes."

"If you see Mme Dorme, ask her when Dannie can call."

She seemed tense, and perhaps was already regretting her initiative. I think she was tempted to hold me back.

"I'll wait for you at the bridge. It's better if I don't stay here in front of the building."

And she indicated the bridge that slices through the tip of Ile Saint-Louis.

I went through the entrance and stopped in front of a huge double-door on my left, made of light-coloured wood. I rang the bell. No-one answered. I could hear no sound behind the door. And yet, we had seen light peeking through the slits in the shutters. The timer on the hall light ran out. I rang again in the dark. No-one. I stood there in the dark, waiting. I sincerely hoped that someone would finally open the door, that the silence would be broken, and that the lights would come back on. At one point, I pounded on the door with my fists, but the wood was so thick that it barely made a sound. Did I really pound on the door that evening? I've so often dreamed of that scene since then that my dream has become confused with reality. Last night, I was in total darkness, with no reference points, and I was pounding on a door with both fists, as if I had been locked in. I was suffocating. I awoke with a start. Yes, once again, the same dream. I tried to remember whether I had pounded like that on that distant night. In any case, I had rung several more times in the dark, and I had been surprised by the sound of the doorbell, both brittle and crystalline. No-one. Silence.

I groped my way out of the building. She was pacing back and forth on the bridge. She took my arm and gave it a squeeze. She was relieved that I was back, and I wondered whether we had just been in danger. I told her that no-one had answered the door.

"I never should have sent you in there," she said. "But some-times I still think things are like they were before . . ."

"Before what?"

She shrugged.

We crossed the bridge and followed the quai de la Tournelle. She kept silent, and it wasn't the moment to ask questions. Everything here was calm and reassuring: the ancient build-ing façades, the trees, the lit street lamps, the narrow streets that spilled onto the quay and reminded me of Restif de La Bretonne. Many pages of my black notebook were filled with notes about him. I didn't even feel like asking her anything. I felt light, carefree, happy to be walking along the quay with her that evening, repeating to myself the name Restif de La Bretonne, with its soft, mysterious cadence.

"Jean . . . I want to ask you something . . ."

We were walking by that square, in a recess from the quay, in the middle of which sit tables and tubs of greenery defin-ing the limits of an outdoor café. That evening, they had put parasols on the tables. A summer's night in a little port town in the South. Murmurs of conversation.

"Jean . . . What would you say if I'd done something really serious?"

I have to confess that the question did not alarm me. Perhaps because of her casual tone, as one might recite song lyrics or lines of a poem. And because of her "Jean, what would you say", it was in fact a line of verse that occurred to me: "Say, Blaise, are we really a long way from Montmartre?"

"What would you say if I'd murdered somebody?"

I thought she was joking, or that she'd asked because of the crime novels she often read. In fact, they were all she read. Maybe in one of those novels, a woman asked her boyfriend the same question.

"What would I say? Nothing."

Still today, I would give the same answer. Do we have the right to judge the people we love? If we love them, it's for a reason, and that reason prevents us from judging them – doesn't it?

"Well . . . Not murdered, exactly . . . More like an accident . . ."

"That's reassuring."

She seemed disappointed by my response, and it was only years later that I recognised its glibness and poor unintentional humour.

"Yes . . . an accident . . . it went off by itself . . ."

"Life's full of stray bullets," I said.

I had immediately thought of gunshots. And indeed, she answered:

"That's right . . . stray bullets . . ."

I burst out laughing. She shot me a reproachful glance. Then she squeezed my arm.

"Let's not talk about these depressing things . . . I had a bad dream last night . . . I dreamed I was in a flat and I shot a man in self-defence . . . A horrible man with heavy eyelids . . ."

"Heavy eyelids?"

"That's right . . ."

She was probably still lost in her dream. But it didn't worry me. I had often had the same experience: certain dreams – or rather, certain nightmares – can stick with you all the next day. They blend in with your most ordinary movements, and even if you're sitting with friends at an outdoor café table in the sun, fragments of them still pursue you and adhere to your real life, like a kind of echo or static that you can't clear away. Sometimes that confusion is due to lack of sleep. I felt like telling her as much, to reassure her. We had come as far as Saint-Julien-le-Pauvre. In front of the American bookshop, benches and chairs had been arranged as if at a café terrace, and about a dozen people were sitting there, listening to some jazz leaking from the shop.

"We should go and sit with them," I said. "It'll take your mind off your bad dream . . ."

"You think so?"

But we kept on walking, I don't remember which way. I recall silent avenues over which the leaves of the plane trees formed a vault, the occasional lit window in the building façade, and the Belfort lion keeping watch, eyes fixed towards the south. She had come out of her dream. We sat on the steep flight of steps leading to rue de l'Aude. I heard the nearby sound of running water. She leaned her face close to mine.

"You shouldn't pay any attention to what I said a little while ago . . . Nothing has changed . . . It's just like before . . ."

That summer night, the ripple of a waterfall or fountain, the long stairway cut into the high retaining wall, from which we overlooked the treetops . . . Everything was calm, and I was certain that before us stretched lines vanishing into the future.

One doesn't often return to the southern part of Paris. The area ended up becoming an internal, imaginary landscape, and it seems extraordinary that names like Tombe-Issoire, Glacière, Montsouris or Château de la Reine Blanche can exist in reality, spelled out on city maps. I've never gone back to rue de l'Aude. Except in my dreams. And then, I see it in different seasons. From the windows of my old room it is covered in snow, but if window at the back. I find myself in front of the other door, the one to the ground-floor flat, the door made of heavy, light-coloured wood that a woman named Mme Dorme was supposed to open for me, that July evening when I was with Dannie. I pause a moment before ringing. Sunlight dapples the door. I feel carefree, liberated from remorse or some obscure guilt. It will be like before; or rather, there will never have been a before or after in our lives, no "something serious", no break, no handicap, no original sin – I struggle to find the right words – no weight that we drag around despite our youth and heedlessness. I am about to ring, and the sound will be as crystalline as on that first evening. The two leaves of the door will open with the same languid movement as the carriage entrance and a blonde woman of about fifty, elegantly dressed and with regular features, will say, "Dannie is expecting you in the salon."

Is this woman Mme Dorme? Every time, I wake up asking myself that question, but there's never an answer. She is mentioned in Langlais's file, which provides only a few insignificant details. No photo of her: ". . . alias Mme Dorme, first associated with Paul Milani at 'number 4' rue de Douai . . . Manageress of Buffet 48 . . . and of Etoile-Iéna . . . Said to have purchased several racehorses fifteen years ago . . . Departure for

The concierge heard two gunshots, just before midnight. After about ten minutes, he saw two men and two women leaving the flat, followed by "a young lady" whom he describes in rather precise detail: she had been a frequent visitor to the flat over the past several months, he had spoken with her several times, and she regularly took in post addressed to her under the name "Mireille Sampierry". That was you. The four others arrived roughly an hour later to carry that nameless, faceless man out to the car parked in front of the building. One individual present that evening – a certain Jean Terrail – testified that it was you who fired the gun, but that the weapon belonged to the stranger and he had threatened you with it "brutally and obscenely". No doubt he had been drinking. He's no longer around to say. It's as if he had never existed. We can suppose that you managed to wrest the gun away from him, that you fired, or else that the shots "went off by themselves" because you made too sudden a movement. Two stray bullets? They found the slugs in a room of the flat in the course of their investigation. But who let them in? Mme Dorme? Not much about you in the file. You were never born in Casablanca, as you had told me one evening when we were talking about Aghamouri and the others at the Unic Hôtel who had "close ties" with Morocco, but quite simply in Paris during the war, two years before me. Born of an unknown father and Andrée Lydia Roger, at 7 rue Narcisse-Diaz in the 16th arrondissement. Mirabeau Clinic. But sometime after the war, they report that your mother, Andrée Lydia Roger, was living at 16 rue Vitruve in the 20th. Why that detail, and why the sudden plunge from the affluent 16th arrondissement to the squalid Charonne district? Perhaps only you could have explained. There is no mention of your brother Pierre, whom you often talked about. They know that you had lived on rue Blanche under the name Mireille Sampierry, but they don't say why you used that name. No reference to your room at the Cité Universitaire or the American Pavilion. Or to avenue Victor-Hugo. And yet, I often accompanied you there and waited for you behind the building with two exits. And you always returned with a wad of cash, and I wondered who had given it to you – but that, too, was something they hadn't noticed. Nothing about the little flat on avenue Félix-Faure, either, or La Barberie, the country house in Feuilleuse. They know that you took a room at the Unic Hôtel, according to information provided by "Davin", but they did not seem in much of a hurry to question you, which would have required only a short wait in the foyer, or a simple telephone call from "Davin" to alert them to your presence. They must have dropped the investigation without much ado, and in any case, by the time I was summoned by Langlais, you had already "disappeared". It's down on paper. Disappeared like Mme Dorme, whom they were unable to track down in Switzerland, assuming they even tried.

I don't know whether they did a slapdash job with this investigation or whether the information they keep in their archives on thousands upon thousands of people is always this incomplete, but I confess I was underwhelmed. Until then, I'd always believed they "probed minds and hearts", that their files contained the most minute details of our lives, all of our paltry secrets, and that we were at the mercy of their silence. But what do they really know about the two of us, about you, apart from those stray bullets and that phantom corpse? In the deposition they made me sign beneath the formula "seen and approved", I say almost nothing about you. Or about myself. I told them that we met not long before through a Moroccan student at the Cité Universitaire, and that you were hoping to enrol at the Censier branch of the university. And that we saw each other for barely three months in the Latin Quarter and around Montparnasse, amid the earnest students and old painters with curly hair and velvet jackets who frequented the area. We went to the movies. And to bookstores. I even specified that we took long walks around Paris and in the Bois de

Boulogne. As I answered those questions in that office on the quai de Gesvres, I heard the clacking of the typewriter. Langlais was typing it up himself, with two fingers. Yes, we also went to the cafés on Boul'Mich, and, not having much money, we sometimes ate in the student cafeteria at the Cité Universitaire. And since he had asked how I spent my free time, wanting, he said, to "get a better sense of our personalities", I ended up giving him other details: we frequented the cinematheque on rue d'Ulm and were planning to sign up for the Jeunesses Musicales. When he asked about Aghamouri and the Unic Hôtel, I felt I was on slippery ground. We had met Aghamouri at the Cité Universitaire cafeteria. I honestly thought he was just another student. Moreover, I had gone to pick him up after his classes at Censier several times. No, I would never have guessed he worked for the "Moroccan secret service". But, anyway, that was none of our business. And the Unic Hôtel? No, no, it wasn't Aghamouri who had brought us there. I had heard they let you go upstairs at the Unic even if you were a minor, which I was. That's why we took a room there from time to time, my girlfriend and I. I noticed that Langlais did not type that answer, and that all my lies were apparently of little interest to him.

"So, if I understand you correctly, Ghali Aghamouri never

introduced you and your girlfriend to these individuals: Duwelz, Marciano, Chastagnier and Georges B., alias Rochard?"

"No . . ." I said.

While pecking at the keys with his two index fingers, he recited the sentence in my stead: "The aforementioned Ghali Aghamouri never introduced me to Duwelz, Marciano, Chastagnier and Rochard. My girlfriend and I merely saw them in the foyer of the hotel." Then he smiled at me and shrugged. Perhaps he thought the same as I did: that all these petty details did not especially concern us. Pretty soon, they would no longer matter in our lives. He remained pensive for a long while, his arms folded behind his typewriter, head lowered, and I thought he had forgotten me. And, in a gentle voice, without looking at me, he said, "Did you know your girlfriend did time in La Petite-Roquette two years ago?" Then he smiled at me again. I felt a pang in my heart. "It wasn't as serious as all that . . . She was there for eight months . . ." And he handed me a sheet of paper that I forced myself to read over very quickly, because he was holding it between his thumb and index finger, and I was afraid he would suddenly snatch it back. Lines and words danced before my eyes: ". . . shoplifting in several luxury department stores . . . was picked up on avenue Victor-Hugo carrying a crocodile-skin handbag . . . 'I would go into a store without a handbag. Once inside, I'd choose one and walk out with it . . . same for the coats . . .'"

He put the sheet on his desk, without giving me time to finish. He seemed embarrassed to have shown me such a document. "It wasn't as serious as all that," he repeated. "Kid stuff, really . . . kleptomania . . . You know what they say about kleptomania?" I was amazed that the interrogation had suddenly taken such an ordinary turn, almost like a friendly chat. "A lack of affection. You steal what nobody ever gave you. Was she lacking affection?" He stared at me with his large blue eyes, and I had the impression that he was trying to read my thoughts, and succeeding.

"Now, of course, she's mixed up in something much more serious . . . It happened three months ago . . . Just before you met her . . . There was a homicide."

I must have gone very pale, since the blue eyes that he'd trained on me took on an expression of concern. He seemed to be studying me.

"Of course, we could always consider this an accident . . . two stray bullets . . ."

With a weary movement, he rolled a blank sheet into his typewriter and asked, "Did your girlfriend ever talk to you about an evening that took place last September, in a flat on 46-bis quai Henri-IV in Paris?"

I answered in the negative and, once again, I heard the clacking of the typewriter. Then another question: "Did your girlfriend ever explain to you why she was always changing her name?" I had not known this detail, but even if I had I wouldn't have been overly surprised. I, too, had changed my forename and falsified my birth date to make myself older, of legal age. Anyway, I knew her only as "Dannie". As he typed my answer, I spelled out the name, recalling my mistake when we'd first met.

"Have you had any word from her since she disappeared and do you have any idea where she might be now?"

That question made me so sad that I couldn't speak. He answered for me, pecking at the keys of his typewriter with his two index fingers: "I have had no word from my girlfriend since she disappeared, and I assume she went abroad . . ."

He interrupted himself:

"Did she ever mention a Mme Dorme to you?"

"No."

He thought for a moment, then continued aloud, still typing with his two fingers:

". . . that she went abroad, probably in the company of the abovementioned Hélène Méreux, alias Mme Dorme."

He heaved a sigh, as if he had just rid himself of a burdensome chore. He handed me the sheet.

"Sign there."

I, too, was relieved to be done with this.

"It's a routine investigation that's been dragging on for months," he said, as if to reassure me. "They'll almost certainly bury the case . . . The corpse supposedly died of natural causes in his home. I hope there won't be any fallout for you. But you never know . . ."

I tried to find a few friendly words before taking my leave.

"You type up the depositions?" I asked. "I was under the impression they were all taken down by hand, back in the day."

"That's right, they were. And most of the inspectors at the time had beautiful handwriting. And they composed their reports in flawless French."

He led me down the hall and we descended the stairs together. Before parting company, at the doorway that opened onto the quay, he said:

"I gather you've started writing as well. By hand?"

"Yes. By hand."

*

They tore down La Petite-Roquette. In its place stretches a public park. When I was about twenty, I often used to visit a certain Adolfo Kaminsky, a photographer who lived in one of the tall buildings across the street. His windows overlooked the hexagonal prison with its six turrets. It was the same period as when you were incarcerated there, but I didn't know it at the time. The other night, I waited at the front gate of the prison, opposite Kaminsky's building, and they let me in. They led me to the visiting room. They had me sit before a glass screen, and you were sitting on the other side. I was talking to you and you seemed to understand me, but although you moved your lips, pressed your forehead against the glass, I couldn't hear your voice. I asked you questions: "Who was Mme Dorme? The phantom corpse from quai Henri-IV? And the person you often went to see in the building with two exits while I waited?" From the movement of your lips, I could see that you were trying to answer, but the glass between us muffled your voice. The silence of an aquarium.

I remember that we often strolled in the Bois de Boulogne. It was late in the afternoon, on days when I had to wait for her behind the building on avenue Victor-Hugo. I will never know why she exited on that side and not through the main entrance, as if she were afraid of running into someone at that time of day. We followed the avenue up to La Muette. As we walked on the path along the lakes, I felt as if a weight had lifted. So did she: she said she'd like it if we could live in a room in one of those rows of buildings bordering the woods. A neutral zone, cut off from everything, among infrequent neighbours whose language we couldn't even understand, so that we wouldn't have to talk to them or answer their questions. We wouldn't be accountable to anyone. Eventually we would forget those black holes of Paris: the Unic Hôtel, La Petite-Roquette, the ground floor on the quay with its corpse, all those evil places that made both of us walk on eggshells.

One late afternoon in October, the sky was already dark, and around us floated a smell of dead leaves, wet earth and stables. We were walking along the Jardin d'Acclimatation and had arrived at the edge of the Saint-James pond. We sat on a bench. I was brooding about the manuscript I'd left in the country house. She had told me we could never go back there. It would be dangerous. But she didn't specify what sort of danger. She had kept the keys to the country house, as she had the ones to the flat on avenue Félix-Faure, though she should have given them back a long time ago. I suspected she might even have made copies unbeknownst to the owners. No doubt she was afraid someone would catch us in the house like thieves.

"Don't fret about it, Jean. We'll get your manuscript back one of these days." She added that I was giving myself a lot of worry over nothing. All I had to do was poke through second-hand booksellers' bins and choose one of those old novels whose few readers were long dead, and which living readers had never heard of. And copy it over. By hand. And say that we had written it.

"What do you think of my idea, Jean?"

I didn't know what to say. I recalled the opening sentence of my manuscript: "Return I must to a time in my youth when they called me the False Knight of Warwick . . ." I thought that with the help of my black notebook, I could rewrite and improve those lost pages. So in the end, she was right: it would almost feel as if I were copying them. By hand. That's what I'm doing today.

She pressed against me and repeated in a murmur, "Don't fret about it, Jean . . ."

Sometime later, one morning, I found an envelope that had been slid under the door to my room:

Jean,
I'm leaving, and this time it's likely we won't see each other for a long while. I won't tell you where I'm going

because I don't yet know myself. Wherever it is, you won't find me. It will be far away – not Paris, in any case. I'm leaving because I don't want you to get in any trouble on my account . . .

   P.S.: I told you a little white lie that's been bothering me. I'm not 21, as I said. I'm 24. So you see, soon I'll be an old lady.

She had copied the letter from a tattered novel that we'd bought one afternoon on the quays. I can still hear her telling me, "Don't fret about it, Jean . . ." The Bois de Boulogne, the empty avenues, the dark mass of the buildings, a lit window that makes you feel you've neglected to turn off the lights in another life, or that someone is still expecting you . . . You must be hiding out in one of those neighbourhoods. Under what name? Sooner or later I'll find the street. But every day the hours grow shorter, and every day I tell myself it will be for another time.

PATRICK MODIANO was born in Paris in 1945. His first novel, *La Place de l'étoile*, was published in 1968 when he was just twenty-two and his works have now been translated into more than thirty languages around the world. He won the Austrian State Prize for European Literature in 2012, the 2010 Prix Mondial Cino Del Duca from the Institut de France for lifetime achievement, the 1978 Prix Goncourt for *Rue des boutiques obscures*, and the 1972 Grand Prix du roman de l'Académie française for *Les boulevards de ceinture*. He was awarded the Nobel Prize in Literature in 2014.

MARK POLIZZOTTI is the translator of more than forty books from the French, including works by Gustave Flaubert, Marguerite Duras, Jean Echenoz and Raymond Roussel. His articles and reviews have appeared in the *Wall Street Journal* and *The Nation*. He is Publisher and Editor-in-Chief at the Metropolitan Museum of Art and lives in Brooklyn, New York.